For the strong, empowered women who embody the heroines I like to create.

Know what you want and strive to get it. Be bold. Be courageous. Be true to yourself.

Nicola Marsh is a *USA TODAY* bestselling and multi-award-winning author who loves nothing better than losing herself in a story. A physiotherapist in a previous life, she now divides her time between raising two dashing heroes, whipping up delish meals, cheering on her footy team and writing—her dream job. And she chats on social media. A lot. Come say hi! Instagram, Twitter, Facebook—she's there! Also find her at nicolamarsh.com.

If you liked *Play Thing* why not try

Look at Me by Cara Lockwood
King's Price by Jackie Ashenden
Unleashed by Caitlin Crews

Also by Nicola Marsh

Hot Sydney Nights

Sweet Thing
Wild Thing

Discover more at millsandboon.co.uk.

PLAY THING

NICOLA MARSH

MILLS & BOON

First Published in Great Britain 2018
by Mills & Boon, an imprint of HarperCollins*Publishers*
1 London Bridge Street, London, SE1 9GF

© 2018 Nicola Marsh

ISBN: 978-0-263-93237-9

MIX
Paper from
responsible sources
FSC C007454

This book is produced from independently certified FSC™ paper
to ensure responsible forest management.
For more information visit www.harpercollins.co.uk/green.

Printed and bound in Spain
by CPI, Barcelona

CHAPTER ONE

CHARLOTTE WAITED UNTIL the boss from hell hung up before slamming down the phone and sticking out her tongue. Childish, but it made her feel good.

She glared at the phone, wishing it would disintegrate so she wouldn't have to talk to him again. Yeah, like that would help. She also had an inbox full of emails from Mr Alexander Bronson, asshole extraordinaire.

The guy was demanding, arrogant and clearly had been put on this earth to make her life a misery.

As if to emphasise the point, an email pinged into her inbox with a gut-churning subject line: One last thing.

Sighing, she opened the email. And stopped breathing.

Forgot to mention, Charlie, I'll be arriving at the Sydney office tomorrow to follow up on my ideas to reconfigure staff. I look forward to meeting you then.

He didn't sign off. He didn't need to. Superior beings from other planets were above mere mortals.

Alexander Bronson, here, in the flesh, tomorrow. Torturing her. Tormenting her. Teasing her.

Charlie. No one ever called her that. She hated it. She'd told him so. Which ensured he never called her anything else. No Miss Baxter for him. Uh-uh. The CEO of countless accountancy firms around Australia, the wunderkind who took ailing companies and turned them around, had an informality about him that won friends and influenced lowly accountants like her.

The kicker was, her boss might be demanding and expect perfection, yet she couldn't help but admire his work ethos. She respected him for it, she identified with hard work. It was all she knew in her lacklustre life. Which made it all the more annoying that a small part of her looked forward to their daily phone calls and his infernal teasing.

Could she be any more pathetic? The highlight of her day was talking to her cocky boss who seemed to make it his life's work to tease some kind of response out of her.

Her cell rang and she glanced at the screen, dithering about whether to take the call. She adored her Aunt Dee but she couldn't cope with any outlandish requests today. She had to prepare for her imminent meeting with the charming Mr Bronson tomorrow.

Mentally chastising her goody-two-shoes conscience, she picked up the cell and stabbed at the answer button.

'Hey, Aunt Dee, I'm at work so can't talk long—'

'Dear girl, I know you're at work.' Her aunt sounded breathless, like she'd jogged up a flight of stairs. Unlikely, considering Dee equated exercise with the devil's work. 'But I need your help and it's urgent.'

Charlotte instantly felt guilty that she'd contemplated ignoring her aunt. Dee had raised her when her flaky parents couldn't be bothered, preferring to travel the world in search of the next village in dire need of education. Dee rarely asked for favours so the fact she needed help meant this could be serious.

'Sure, whatever you need. Is everything okay?'

Dee inhaled a loud breath. 'Not really. My friend Queenie has had a nasty fall and broken her hip. She's alone, with no one to care for her animals, so I need to drive up to Byron Bay now. But the owner of the building where I keep stock for my business is coming to inspect it later today and I need to vacate the lease space.'

Her heart sank. As if this day couldn't get any worse. Sorting through her aunt's questionable 'stock' for her kinky online business wasn't one of her favourite activities on the planet. Aunt Dee had enlisted her help on more than one occasion to stuff envelopes for orders and Charlotte blushed just thinking about some of the apparatus people used in their sex lives.

'You need me to pack everything up and store it at home?'

Dee sighed in relief. 'Could you, sweetie? It would mean I could be at Queenie's today rather than tomorrow and she really needs me.'

Charlotte's inner child wanted to say 'I need you' but that was selfish and untrue. She'd learned from an early age to depend on no one but herself. She valued her independence, wore it like a badge of honour. Except that lately, her closest friends Abby and Mak had found great guys, leaving her to ponder whether being alone was something she cherished because she could or because she had to.

Shaking off her melancholy, she said, 'Leave everything to me.'

'You're a lifesaver, Charlotte.' Dee made smooching

sounds. 'Not sure how long I'll be gone, maybe a few weeks. I'll let you know.'

'Okay—' but Dee had already hung up, leaving Charlotte to face the inevitable.

An afternoon of packing up vibrators, nipple clamps and edible underwear.

Oh, goody.

CHAPTER TWO

ALEXANDER BRONSON HADN'T been back in Sydney for a year and as he traversed the Harbour Bridge he couldn't help but glance at the Opera House on his left and remember the first time he'd been there. The first time he'd felt like he'd finally broken free of the shackles of his past.

Sydney had a unique vibe, far removed from his claustrophobic upbringing in outback New South Wales. It was the city where he'd studied, where he'd launched his career, where he'd ensured he'd never have to end up like his father.

His unofficial home, a boutique hotel in the Central Business District, beckoned. But first he had to check out his last property for the day, a warehouse on the outskirts of the glitzy eastern suburbs. He'd already been to Manly, Mosman and Balmoral Beach today, ensuring his investments were running smoothly. This last warehouse had to be cleared asap for a new tenant to move in tomorrow and his manager had informed him there'd been some kind of hold-up.

He didn't suffer incompetence lightly. He liked order in all aspects of life. Which was why he'd sort out this complication today and face the shake-up at The Number Makers tomorrow.

Crazy name for an accountancy firm. Then again, considering the mess the initial owner had made of the business, it didn't surprise him. Thank goodness for workers like Charlotte Baxter. Working offsite could be tough, but she'd made everything much easier than expected. He admired her work ethic, the way she questioned him and proposed solutions to problems he might not have anticipated.

He also liked the way she brought out the worst in him.

She sounded so prim and proper, so damned disapproving, he couldn't help but tease her.

He shouldn't make assumptions but he knew her type. Conservative wardrobe. Conservative views. Conservative life. She probably had an equally reserved husband, well-behaved kids and knitted on her lunch break. Though this was at odds with the fact that he'd registered her marital status as single when he'd dug deeper into his rising-star employee.

He'd deliberately called her Charlie during their first call and she hadn't hesitated in reprimanding him—ensuring he never called her anything but. Because there was an underlying hint of playfulness in her sharp reprimands and retorts, as if she wanted to cut loose but didn't know how.

Not that he was the guy to help her do it, but if he could make his work environment more pleasant, he was all for it. He'd had enough of morose, stifled environments back home to ensure he went out of his way to foster the opposite in all aspects of his life ever since.

Oh, yeah, he was looking forward to meeting the woman who'd smoothed his entry into the company. He had grand plans for her. Management plans. Because The Number Makers needed to be turned into a profitable business again and that meant appointing qualified staff. Staff like his introverted Charlie.

He couldn't wait to meet her.

CHAPTER THREE

CHARLOTTE STEPPED INTO her aunt's rented space in a cavernous warehouse and immediately wished she'd said no to helping out.

She wasn't a prude, but seeing evidence of how much fun other people had in their sex lives always made her feel lacking somehow.

Her aunt's online business, Dee's Delights, did a roaring trade in all things sexy. From dildos to condoms, beads to fetish wear, her aunt dealt in it all. And if the lavish lifestyle her aunt enjoyed was any indication, many people were return customers.

Dee had told her about the business when Charlotte turned eighteen. Initially mortified that her aunt even knew what a cock ring was, Charlotte had studiously ignored anything to do with her aunt's line of work. Now, at the ripe old age of twenty-five, and never having had a long-term boyfriend, Charlotte wondered if having to handle all this stuff today was the universe's way of telling her to lighten the hell up.

Thankfully, most of the raunchier stuff still resided in boxes, leaving her to pack only the vibrators, handcuffs and lingerie. She'd booked a courier for six tonight, meaning she had three hours to get every box filled and taped.

As she held up a pair of fluffy fuchsia handcuffs and smirked, she glimpsed a full-length mirror on the inside of a partially open wardrobe door. Probably a remnant of the last tenant—she couldn't imagine her aunt wanting to try on any of her merchandise and didn't want to—but the moment the idea of trying stuff on popped into her head she couldn't dislodge it.

Her gaze fell on the lingerie. A turquoise chemise with lace overlay. A purple halter baby-doll. A wet-look corset. A pink body stocking. An ebony faux-leather bustier and thong.

Heat flushed her cheeks as she picked up the latter and held it up. Would her sedate life change if she wore stuff like this? Not that anybody would see it, but it might give her more confidence to shake things up a little. And she wanted that, craved that, with every cell in her lonely body.

Her flatmate Mak had jetted off to New York with her delectable guy Hudson last week, leaving her more alone than ever. Charlotte rarely dated, didn't go out clubbing and preferred reading to sexting. On the odd occasion she dipped her toes into the dating pool, she went for boring guys like…her. Because ultimately, that was the kind of guy she could see herself marrying, having kids with and with whom she could build the kind of life she'd never had. Secure and happy, with a house she could grow old in, surrounded by a family of her own making.

She'd found the house but wasn't having much luck with the guy.

Before she could second-guess her crazy decision she pulled the elastic off her ponytail and ran her fingers through her hair. She took off her glasses, toed off her flat pumps, unbuttoned her white shirt and unzipped her grey pencil skirt. The warehouse air had a chill, making her skin pebble as she stripped off her sensible cotton underwear. Or maybe her goosebumps had more to do with the naughty thrill of slipping on the thong and bungling her way into the bustier with detachable lace collar.

When she'd done up the last hook, she took a deep breath and padded over to the wardrobe. Opened the door wider. Took a peek in the mirror. And gasped.

Her reflection didn't shock her as much as the sight of a tall gorgeous guy in a suit staring at her with obvious appreciation.

'Who the hell are you and what are you doing here?' She spun around, covering her bits even though they weren't really exposed.

Her handbag and cell were on the table laden with boxes, too far away to make an emergency call if she had to.

Damn, why had she been so stupid? She could've dressed up—or undressed in this case—in her flat where she'd be storing the boxes, not here where any pervert could wander in.

'I could ask you the same question,' the handsome stranger said, stepping inside the room and closing the door.

Uh-oh.

Being alone in an empty warehouse in raunchy underwear with a man, no matter how attractive, wasn't good. She had more sense than this. She blamed her stupid impulsiveness on the realisation that her life was so empty she actually looked forward to verbally sparring with her irritating boss daily.

She'd wanted to cut loose for just one moment. To feel what other women felt wearing underwear like this. She hadn't banked on having an audience for a foolish moment of bravado.

'Get out,' she yelled, sidling towards her clothes, fear making her heart pound in her ears.

'I own this place so that's not going to happen.' His curious gaze fell on the table, where the vibrators and lingerie lay scattered. 'You, on the other hand, need to tell me what you're doing here and why my warehouse has turned into a sex shop.'

There was something vaguely familiar about his condescending tone and she hoped to God he wasn't a client whose taxes she'd done.

'Don't be ridiculous, this isn't a sex shop. My aunt rents this space, from you apparently, for her online business and she asked me to pack everything up so the new tenant can move in tomorrow.' She gestured at the merchandise, belatedly realising she'd left herself exposed when a glimmer of interest lit his gaze. 'So if you leave me to it, I'll be out of here in a few hours.'

'Well, aren't you the little helper,' he drawled, his gaze starting at her toes and working its way upward, a slow, leisurely perusal that made her nipples harden.

Her body's reaction startled her. She'd never reacted to any man like this before, let alone a stranger. She read about this kind of thing in the romance novels she devoured by the boxful: the shy woman instantly attracted to the commanding man. It was a seduction game she fantasised about but knew could never happen to her. They called those novels fiction for a reason.

Yet here she was, standing in front of a guy she didn't know, letting him look his fill. And enjoying it.

When he reached her eyes, what she saw made her knees wobble a tad. Desire. Passion. Lust. The kind of lust she'd never, ever seen in a man's eyes when they looked at her.

'Is trying on every outfit part of you *helping* out?'

His obvious desire discombobulated her and when he grinned the smug smile of a guy who knew exactly the effect he had on her, she made an impulsive decision to make him pay. She might be inexperienced and naive when it came to sparring with a man but that didn't mean he could toy with her.

'My old corsets and bustiers are worn out so I thought I'd replenish my stocks.' A blush heated her cheeks at the blatant lie but once she started she couldn't stop. 'It's a tough job looking this good for the men of Sydney but somebody's gotta do it.'

He laughed, a rich, deep rumble that reached down into her chest and filled the lonely ache that resided there.

'Does that include me, considering I'm a man and I'm in Sydney?'

Charlotte had never played games with any guy. She didn't flirt and she didn't elicit grand passion in them. But something about this stranger made her feel like she could do both.

'Why, do you think I look good?' She rested her hands on her hips in a blatant invitation for him to look his fill again, wondering what magic powers the lingerie held to make her this bold.

'Honey, you have no idea.' He stalked towards her and her newfound bravado fled. She edged towards the table, needing her cell within reach. But like an eternal klutz she stumbled and would have fallen if he hadn't been by her side in a second. Strong hands steadied her, held her upright, made her yearn for things she had no right to crave.

Up close, he was even more startlingly good-looking: dark wavy hair, blue eyes the colour of Bondi on a clear day, chiselled jaw dusted with the faintest hint of stubble, the perfection marred by a small scar on the underside of his chin. And when he smiled again…oh, boy, she felt it all the way down to her toes and a few choice places in between.

She cleared her throat, trying to summon outrage at being held by a stranger while dressed like a stripper. 'Let me go.'

But her command sounded soft and uncertain, falling flat if his amused smirk was any indication.

'Do you want me to?'

He quirked an eyebrow, daring her to deny the invisible energy zapping between them.

She couldn't explain it. She didn't do casual sex; could count the number of times she'd actually had sex on one hand because it had been unremarkable. She didn't believe in instant attraction or one-night stands. Or having vertical sex with a hot stranger in a warehouse.

This wasn't her.

But what if it could be?

For a moment, she wondered where that voice had come from. Her conscience didn't encourage her to go wild. Quite the opposite, in fact.

And where had it got her? Alone and craving a relationship.

What if she did something so out of character that
she could never go back to the person she was? Would
that give her the kick-start she needed to *make* the life
she wanted happen instead of *waiting* for it to happen
to her?

'I don't know you... I mean, I'm not good at this...and
I don't usually do this kind of thing with strangers—'

He kissed her. His lips were commanding, his skill
obvious in the way he exacted the right amount of
pressure—not too hard, not too soft...

A kiss to her meant a meshing of lips, the occasional
tongue, a bit messy and nothing to rave about.

What this guy could do with his tongue...the moment it invaded her mouth and touched hers she couldn't
think. Couldn't breathe. Couldn't do anything but hold
onto his lapels and press against him, desperate for
contact.

His relentless assault on her lips made her tremble
with longing. He changed the pressure, he nipped her
bottom lip so hard it bordered on painful, and then he
soothed it with a seductive sweep of his tongue.

A fleeting thought pierced her passion haze: could
a woman orgasm from a kiss? Because she throbbed
so startlingly from his mouth on hers that it had to be
scientifically possible.

His fingers threaded through her hair, grazing her
scalp, and she moaned at the tingling sensation it elicited. He took it as a sign of encouragement, spinning
her around and hoisting her onto the table. She gasped
at the cold plastic against her bare butt and he broke
their kiss to stare at her in wide-eyed wonder.

'I don't do this. Sex with a stranger.'

'Me either,' she said, breathless and slightly husky. Wishing he hadn't stopped. Wishing she had the guts to articulate how badly she wanted him to continue.

His hungry gaze locked on her, daring her to follow through on what they'd started. 'So what do you want to do?'

He'd given her an out.

She should take it.

Her entire life revolved around rational, well-considered decisions. Weighing up facts. Making safe choices.

Where had it got her?

Single and not loving it. Her sex life was lived vicariously through erotic romance novels, craving an elusive something that would jolt her staid life; something like this crazy, exciting interlude to give her confidence a boost and ensure she could follow through on finding her perfect guy.

Staring into this guy's amazing blue eyes, she wondered if maybe karma had delivered exactly what she needed.

Her throat tightened but she had to get the words out, had to take a chance for once. 'I want to do this.'

Before her common sense kicked in, she placed her hand on his abs. Low enough to be suggestive. High enough he could end this now and walk away if he wanted to.

His low groan raised the fine hairs on her arms as he nudged her knees apart, stepped between them and slid his hands under her butt, sliding her towards him.

She gasped as he ground against her, hard and insistent, while his hands palmed her breasts. The softest whimper filled the air and through a hazy fog of want, she realised it had come from her.

She wrapped her legs around him and he responded by rolling her nipples between his thumbs and forefingers, making her go a little crazy. She writhed against him, wanting more. He plucked at her nipples, sending a sizzle to her core.

If his touch felt so good with the stupid faux leather as a barrier, what would it feel like to be naked? She wanted to find out but he had other ideas.

'Lie back,' he said, placing a palm between her breasts and gently pushing. 'Prop on your elbows so I can see you.'

The guys Charlotte had been with didn't issue orders. They got the basics done without a word.

She liked being told what to do. Liked the gleam in his eyes when she did exactly as he wanted. She eased back until she rested on her elbows, uncertainty making her shiver as he hooked his thumbs under the elastic of the thong. He tugged gently, lowering it, leaving her naked and vulnerable.

She'd never felt so exposed. But her protest died on her lips as he locked gazes with her at the same time he slid a finger inside her.

Reverence widened his eyes, as if she'd bestowed a great gift on him, and her flutters of worry faded beneath his ministrations.

Another finger slipped inside her, rhythmically sliding in and out as his thumb circled her clitoris. Slow. Steady. He was driving her insane with the feel of him and the way he met her gaze. Uncompromising. Confident in his ability to satisfy her. Seeing her, really *seeing* her.

'You are so frigging beautiful,' he muttered, his tone barely above a growl, and she gritted her teeth to stop from groaning out loud as the pleasure built. She tensed her muscles and began spiralling out of control. She blanked her mind until all she could focus on was him. His touch. His fingers. His stare.

Her orgasm crashed over her, so strong, so unexpected, wiping her out. She couldn't hold back, her yell loud and triumphant.

She expected to be swamped with mortification the second her body stopped pulsating. But nothing happened, other than a relentless yearning to do it all again.

'Thank you,' she murmured, sounding oddly formal.

'You're welcome.' His smile widened as he reached down and unzipped. 'If you want, there's more where that came from.'

Charlotte's jaw dropped open. She'd heard of the fabled internal orgasm but equated it to other fanciful, elusive things, like unicorns and fairies.

Apparently her mystery man believed in all things mystical and she watched in unabashed fascination as he unsnapped his trousers and pushed them down along with his jocks.

Showing her proof of exactly why he could be so confident.

Wowza. She might not have seen many erect penises but the ones she had made this one look like a giant. With a wicked-looking head.

She smiled at her joke and he quirked an eyebrow.

'It doesn't bode well that you take one look at me and want to laugh.'

A killer sense of humour and a big dick. She'd hit the jackpot. Ding, ding, ding.

'I'm out of my comfort zone here. Can't you give a girl a break?'

'Thought I already had.' He winked and she laughed, surprised at how easy this felt.

The few other times she'd had sex had been awkward, without a hint of banter. She liked this, liked feeling like a wanton goddess splayed before a sex god.

'This is crazy. You know that, right?'

He nodded, fishing a condom from his wallet and rolling it on with an expertise that indicated he'd done it many times before. 'Crazy is good.'

He set about proving it, sliding into her with a force that made her gasp. He grabbed her butt, lifting it slightly so he could drive into her on an angle that ensured he hit that fabled sweet spot. He thrust into her over and over with a relentless force that had her surging up, reaching for him.

She held onto his shoulders as he half lifted her off the table, his penetration deeper, his rhythm faster. The pleasure bordered on pain and she bit his shoulder as she came again, stunned by the ferocity of it.

He tensed and groaned a second later, his fingers digging into her butt so hard she might not be able to sit for a week. She didn't care. She didn't care about anything other than this euphoria making her feel as if she could do anything.

He held her for what seemed like an eternity before gently lowering her to the table and withdrawing. She felt the loss immediately. Craved more. Mentally chastised herself for being stupid.

He turned away, giving her time to put her clothes on while he took care of business. She didn't like seeing his back. Not when their fronts had connected so well.

Remorse, swift and stabbing, flooded her.

What the hell had she been thinking, having sex with a stranger?

However, when he turned back to her, his expression open, his smile satisfied, she couldn't be sorry.

'You were incredible.' He cupped her face between his hands and brushed a soft kiss across her lips.

To Charlotte's horror, the burn of impending tears stung her eyes and she blinked, forcing a smile as she pushed him away.

'So were you,' she said, sounding flippant, while inside a little part of her crumbled at his unexpected tenderness. 'But I really need to get this tidied up now.'

It was a curt dismissal he didn't deserve but she had to get him out of here before she cried.

'Sure, I hear the landlord is a slavedriver.' He seemed completely unfazed by her rudeness but he stared at her with a newfound intensity that bordered on uncomfortable. 'Maybe I'll see you around?'

'Maybe,' she ground out, refraining from adding, 'like never.'

Scorching sex with a stranger hadn't been on her to-do list today but now that it had happened…did she feel different? More confident? More womanly? Just *more*?

She had no freaking idea because in seizing the moment, she'd moved so far out of her comfort zone she'd ended up on another planet, one where good girls did bad things and didn't regret it. Especially when that bad thing had been oh, so good.

But no matter how incredible her momentary lapse had been, it couldn't happen again. She needed to move on and refocus on the priorities in her life. Like finding a genuine guy who'd want more than a quickie on a table in the back room of a warehouse.

He paused at the door, as if he wanted to say something. Ask for her phone number? Ask her out to dinner? Her inner romantic yearned for some gesture to indicate that this hadn't been just sex to him.

She should have been relieved when he half shrugged and held up a hand in farewell before closing the door behind him.

She wasn't. All she could think was that she'd found the bad boy she'd been craving but had let him go far too easily.

CHAPTER FOUR

ALEX HAD DONE something bad.

The kind of bad that could get him a lifetime membership to hell alongside the naughty guy with horns and a pitchfork, ensuring he danced on hot coals for all eternity.

On his first day back in Sydney, he'd envisaged having a quiet afternoon inspecting his property investments.

He hadn't expected to have sex with the woman he'd earmarked to take The Number Makers into the future.

Even now, hunkered behind a solid wooden door in a rather ugly office, he couldn't believe he'd been stupid enough to have sex with Charlotte Baxter.

Not that he'd recognised her until it was too late, with her hair down, no glasses and wearing the kind of lingerie to fuel wet dreams.

Because the woman he'd researched online once he'd taken this job looked nothing like the woman he'd had scorching sex with in that warehouse.

The headshot on The Number Makers website depicted a prim woman wearing a bland white blouse, minimal make-up, steel-rimmed glasses and a dorky headband, with her hair pulled tight in a high ponytail.

Never in his wildest dreams had he expected Charlotte to be wearing leather underwear and looking nothing like her picture when they first met.

There'd been a vague familiarity about her at the time, but he'd put it down to wishful thinking. His little head overriding his big one because he'd wanted to get laid and the intriguing woman in the leather underwear had seemed up for it.

It wasn't until they'd done the deed that the truth had detonated. The moment he'd heard her say, 'I really need to get this tidied up now,' he'd known.

Charlotte had used that same phrase many times over the last few weeks when he'd assigned her tasks. Usually in reference to cleaning up work, where she had to deal with the mess left by the old manager.

When it came to work, she'd always been agreeable. It was only when he tried to be friendly, to get to know her better, that she became abrupt and shut him down.

I really need to get this tidied up now.

Fuck. He'd been struck dumb when he'd realised he'd slept with an employee. That was when he'd taken a closer look and realised that without the uptight hairdo and the glasses, she had the same eyes. A captivating slate grey that held secrets.

Like the fact she could masquerade as a vixen after hours once she shed her librarian persona.

He should have trusted his gut that she looked vaguely familiar, should have taken a closer look at her face. Unfortunately, he'd taken one look at her lithe body and lost it. Not because she was a bombshell—she had small, pert breasts thrust heavenward by that saucy bustier, a trim waist, slim legs and an ass that fitted in his hands nicely.

No, he'd lost it because he'd seen something in her eyes…a wistful yearning, a war waged between boldness and fear, like she wanted to jump him but didn't know how.

It had captured his interest like nothing else.

After he'd realised her true identity, he hadn't been able to get over the startling contrast between the woman he'd imagined and the woman who'd made him hard by fixing those cool grey eyes on him.

He could read most people. But after he'd twigged that he'd screwed Charlotte, he couldn't fathom how the hell she'd been so into it. How did a no-nonsense woman switch from being contained at work to confident enough to strip down, try on raunchy underwear and fuck a stranger in a warehouse? It left him completely baffled.

She'd intrigued him during their many phone conversations and he'd wanted to see how far he could push her. He'd deliberately teased her over the last few weeks, chuckling at the curt shutdowns she reserved for him—and probably every male on the planet.

To think how she'd responded to his touch…at the time, he hadn't been able to explain rationally his over-the-top urge to possess her. Sure, he'd been too busy to date lately and hadn't had sex in three months, but he'd never been driven by urges before. Celibacy didn't bother him, especially when he had a new job in the pipeline. Yet he'd taken one look at Charlotte—not that he'd known it was her at the time—and wanted her.

His cock hardened and he shifted in the uncomfortable ergonomic chair. First item of business on the agenda at The Number Makers: change the furniture and make it more comfortable for staff so they wanted to stick around and work.

Though when he met Charlotte in a few minutes' time and she realised who she'd had scorching sex with on a table in a back room of his warehouse, he had a feeling nothing would make her stick around.

He had to convince her otherwise.

Her work spoke for itself. She went above and beyond for her clients. She put in extra hours without expecting remuneration. She carried the load for her team. And she'd completed every task he'd set for her over the last few weeks. He'd been testing her, seeing how willing she was to take on extra work and she'd passed.

He hoped to God she wouldn't quit because he hadn't kept his dick in his pants.

Worse, he couldn't get the image of her splayed on that table out of his head. He'd never seen anything so damned erotic as a woman he'd just met being so willing and eager. She'd been absolutely wanton and it had turned him on big time. Later, when he'd discovered her identity, it had made him wonder how he could have gotten her so wrong. Had that bold, fiery woman always been hidden beneath her brusque exterior? And if so, what would it be like to coax her to come out and play again?

He couldn't afford to think that way. He'd made a mistake by sleeping with an employee, a mistake he had no intention of replicating.

But the fact he couldn't stop thinking about her, had lain awake most of last night because of it, didn't bode well for when she entered this office shortly.

He needed to focus on work. On making The Number Makers a strong, viable company. The more money he made, the further he left his old life behind. He couldn't afford a slip-up.

But what if he'd already slipped up in slaking his unexpected lust for her?

CHAPTER FIVE

CHARLOTTE LIKED TICKING off tasks in her head.

Pack up Aunt Dee's merchandise? Check.

Have the boxes couriered to her flat? Check.

Enjoy sizzling sex with random stranger? Check.

Even now, the next morning, heat surged to her cheeks every time she thought about what she'd done in that warehouse.

She, the queen of introverts, having two mind-blowing orgasms with a guy whose name she didn't even know.

It had been preposterous. Ludicrous. And so freaking incredible that she'd found herself smiling at random times last night, and several times first thing this morning.

After he'd left and she'd got over her funk at doing something so completely illogically bizarre, she'd expected embarrassment and shame to follow her initial remorse. It hadn't happened. Instead, she'd felt oddly empowered, like she'd taken control of her sexuality and wielded it in a way she'd never anticipated.

Of course it hadn't lasted and by the time she'd got home, her newfound boldness had faded and humiliation had set in.

How could she have done that?

Obsessing about sex with a stranger was the last thing she needed, especially when she had to meet her pain-in-the-ass boss in person for the first time in ten minutes.

Her confidence had taken more hits than a boxer over the years and while her sexy encounter yesterday had given her a momentary boost, she'd reverted to type today, envisaging their first meeting to be more of the usual: him demanding, her deferent.

To give herself confidence she'd dressed to impress today, wearing her version of a power suit. A deep burgundy knee-length skirt, an ivory silk blouse that tied in a bow at the neck, a fitted black jacket and low kitten heels. She'd even gone all out and straightened her hair. Not in any effort to impress Alexander bloody Bronson but to ensure she exuded self-assurance when she faced her nemesis.

Okay, so she was being a tad overdramatic, but he'd really riled her these last few weeks, barking orders, demanding perfection and teasing her with that ridiculous nickname. Charlie. Made her sound like a boy. And hit a little too close to home because of how asexual she felt at times, languishing in her single life and wishing things could be different. That *she* could be different.

Courtesy of that sexy stranger yesterday, maybe she could be.

That was what her brain-fade in that warehouse had ultimately been about: embracing her dormant sexy side, indulging in a little excitement, seeing exactly what she was capable of if she let go a little. Because, although she craved a stable, loving guy, deep down she wanted him to rock her world in more ways than one.

Trying not to cringe with embarrassment at the indignity of having sex with a man whose name she didn't know, she gathered her files, checked them for the third time to ensure she'd stacked them in alphabetical order then rested her electronic tablet on the top, ready to show Mr Bronson exactly how competent she could be.

She hadn't seen him arrive but the receptionist assured her he'd been holed up in the old manager's office since early this morning and hadn't opened his door since.

She'd be the first staff member he would interview.

'Woo-hoo, lucky me,' she muttered, glancing at the old-fashioned round clock opposite her desk. She valued punctuality so surely her new boss would be impressed if she arrived five minutes early for their meeting?

Not giving herself time to ponder the upcoming face-to-face she'd been dreading ever since he'd told her of his arrival in Sydney, she swept up her work in her arms and headed for his office.

The receptionist mouthed 'good luck' and Charlotte grimaced in response, before knocking twice on Mr Bronson's door.

When she heard a clipped, 'Come in,' she opened the door and stepped inside. He had his back to her, his butt resting on the desk while he spoke into a cell pressed to his ear.

Her first impressions: dark wavy hair a tad too long to be conventional, broad shoulders, designer suit, nice ass.

Wow, that guy yesterday must have really done a number on her if one of the first things she noticed about Mr Tall, Dark and Demanding was his ass.

She closed the door and crossed the room, mentally reciting all the ways she'd like to torture him in response to how he'd tortured her over the last few weeks.

However, all thought fled when he ended his call and turned to face her.

Shock rendered her muscles useless and the files in her hands tumbled to the floor, along with her tablet, the numbness flooding her body soon replaced by something far more sinister.

Soul-deep, soul-destroying mortification.

Because the boss she had to impress to keep this job, the boss who'd made her life hell with his demands, the boss who could make or break this company, was the sexy guy who'd turned her world upside down yesterday in the warehouse.

CHAPTER SIX

WHEN ALEX TOOK on a new client he threw himself into the business of rejuvenating that company one hundred per cent. He'd gained a reputation as astute, driven and results-focused because of it. Clients came to *him* these days. He rarely advertised. And he'd treated The Number Makers job with the same industrious approach. Meaning he'd researched the key players before he started. Meaning he knew Charlotte Baxter was dedicated, conscientious and goal-orientated before she walked through his door.

He also knew she'd probably want to eviscerate him once she got past the shock.

'Need some help?' He didn't wait for a response, moving around the desk to squat and gather up her files. It would give her time to compose herself, as a small part of him felt like a complete bastard for springing a surprise of this magnitude on her when he could have called her last night and warned her.

If he'd been blown away when he'd realised the truth yesterday he could only imagine how she'd be feeling now.

When he stood and placed her files and tablet on the desk, she still hadn't moved but some of her colour had returned.

'Why don't you have a seat and we'll talk?' He laid a hand in the small of her back and she jumped as if he'd electrocuted her.

He didn't know whether to be flattered or appalled.

'I know this is awkward, but it doesn't have to be—'

'You *knew*?' She sank onto the chair opposite, her eyes wide and accusing, her mouth open slightly, shell-shocked. 'I mean, yesterday, when we…you know…you knew who I was?'

Hell.

Alex had intended on coming clean but not this soon. He'd wanted to smooth the way, reassure her that what had happened wouldn't interfere with their working relationship at all. But one look at her mouth twisting in disgust told him he'd be fighting a monstrous battle to convince her to stay, let alone listen.

'Charlie, look—'

'Don't call me that,' she growled. 'Don't you dare call me that.'

She shook her head, sending a sleek fall of hair over one shoulder. He preferred the way she'd looked yesterday, tousled and make-up–free, and the fact she'd gone to so much trouble today to impress her new boss made him feel bad anew.

'Let me explain.' He laid out his hands, palms up, like he had nothing to hide. Yeah, like that would placate her. 'I know I should have said something yesterday. I'm a businessman and I'm good at what I do, so I researched this company before taking on the job.'

Her eyes narrowed, fiery slate slits pinning him with a disdain he deserved. 'What do you want, a medal?'

He bit back his first instinct to laugh. Good to know

she had a sense of humour beneath that austere front. Along with lingerie designed to make a man lose his mind.

'What I'm trying to say is, I didn't recognise you when I set foot in that warehouse. You had your hair down and glasses off and were wearing that lingerie…'

Crap, how could he explain the next bit without sounding like a total sleaze?

'And?' Disgust had given way to audible animosity. He hoped it was an improvement.

'You blew me away and I couldn't control my baser instincts. We had phenomenal sex, but it wasn't until you said something afterward that I realised who you were.'

He could have sworn her upper lip curled in derision. 'And what was that?'

'You said "I really need to get this tidied up now", referring to your aunt's merchandise in the warehouse, but it's a phrase you've used often in reference to tasks I've set you over the last few weeks.'

Her frosty expression didn't change, as if she was unsure whether to believe him or not, but she gave a begrudging nod and he pinched the bridge of his nose, searching for the right words to make her understand. 'I was honest about one thing yesterday. I don't do things like that, meet women and have sex with them in under ten minutes. But seeing you like that…it blew my mind.'

At last, a breakthrough, when her rigid shoulders relaxed a tad. Not a complete thaw but he'd work on it, whatever it took. He needed Charlotte on board for his revamp of this company. And if having to work along-side this intriguing woman while he did it was a side benefit, he was all for it.

'You seriously couldn't control yourself around me?'

Out of all the responses he'd imagined, that wasn't it. She sounded hesitant, slightly awed, as if she couldn't believe he'd want her.

Some asshole must have really done a number on her for her confidence to be that low. It made him want to vault the desk, sweep her into his arms and show her exactly how sexy she was.

'You're incredible, and when I saw you I wanted you.' He shrugged, hoping the simple truth would appease more than an apology. 'And at the risk of having you fling that tablet at my head, seeing you strut in here only reinforces that snap judgement I made yesterday. But I know we have to work together and we're professionals. So let's chalk up yesterday to what it was—phenomenal, impulsive, amazing sex between consulting adults—and move on to business.'

She stared at him, dazed, but the faint pink in her cheeks indicated he'd hit the mark by articulating just how incredible it had been between them.

'You expect us to work together and pretend like nothing happened?'

She'd lost the biting, sarcastic edge and it gave him hope.

'I don't know about you, but I'm not that good a pretender.' He steepled his fingers together and rested them on the desk, trying to project a professional picture, when forgetting what they'd done in that warehouse was the furthest thing from his mind.

Seeing her again, sitting opposite him in her conservative work attire, only made him want to see what was under it all the more. Would she be wearing lace? Satin? Or that risqué leather again?

Damn, not helping the hard-on situation.

'But doing the best job I can for this company is important to me and I want you to work alongside me to achieve that goal. Can you do it?'

He half expected her to tell him to stick his offer. To tender her resignation and sue the pants off him.

Instead, after a long pause where she studied him with disconcerting intensity, she nodded.

'I can do this if you can.'

Hot damn, that almost sounded like a challenge.

As if she thought he couldn't work with her without reverting to the horny caveman he'd been yesterday. He'd show her.

But in agreeing to keep this all business, he'd be deprived of some serious pleasure.

Their first encounter had been colossal.

What would prim Charlotte be like if she really let go?

CHAPTER SEVEN

CHARLOTTE LEFT THE office in a daze. She couldn't return to her desk to focus on work and pretend her carefully ordered world hadn't just been tipped on its head.

She'd had sex with her new boss.

Not just sex. Amazing, stupendous, multi-orgasmic sex. The kind of sex she'd only ever read about but never dreamed could happen for real.

As she walked aimlessly in the bright Sydney sunshine, she remembered one of the last things she'd said to her flatmate Mak before she'd left to take Broadway by storm.

'I need a bad boy. Some big, bold, annoying, arrogant guy to rattle my cage.'

Well, she'd got her wish and then some.

In what weird alternate universe, in what giant cosmic twist of fate, did she have the best sex of her life only to discover she'd have to work alongside the hot guy who'd rocked her world? The guy who held her dream of owning her perfect house in the palm of her hand and had the power to make or break it with a snap of his talented fingers?

It didn't seem possible. But it was and now Alexander Bronson expected her to work with him and act like he hadn't been inside her in the most intimate way?

Impossible. Improbable. Improper.

Because Charlotte couldn't forget, despite what she'd told him.

She blamed him, for saying all that stuff about how badly he'd wanted her and how he couldn't control himself around her. As if she were some glamorous femme fatale who inspired that kind of passion in a man. She wished.

There'd been a moment when she'd first seen him behind his desk, an infinitesimal moment, where she'd seen hunger in his eyes. As if he still wanted her. It should have sent her running. It didn't.

For the simple fact she liked feeling wanted.

Men didn't turn their heads to stare as she walked down the street. She didn't inspire sexist wolf whistles or lewd comments. And the one and only time she'd succumbed to searching for a date online, she'd taken down her profile from the app after a day when she'd received a mortifying two less-than-stellar requests.

Besides, she valued her job. She needed her job. And she couldn't walk away now, not when she was so close to realising one of her long-held dreams.

Having nomadic parents, being raised by a kooky aunt, meant Charlotte craved security like nothing else. And the quirky cottage on the outskirts of Sydney that she'd fallen in love with represented that to her.

A home.

A house all of her own, where she could establish the life she wanted before following the rest of her dreams: a husband, kids, the works. Charlotte wanted it all and knew the only way she could make it happen was to go after it.

It wouldn't be easy, finding her perfect guy. She knew this, considering she'd have to date regularly to discover what she really wanted in a man and her track record in the dating stakes had been abysmal until now. But the house was a first step in the right direction and somehow, with her twisted logic, she thought that once she had the house she could set about finding a guy happy to live in it.

She almost had enough for a deposit, enough for the bank to take her seriously for a hefty loan application. Just another fortnight and she could start living her dream.

But to do so, she had to tolerate working with Alexander Bronson.

'You can do this,' she muttered, kicking at a stone on the footpath, as her cell buzzed in her pocket.

She fished it out, her palms growing clammy as his name popped up on the screen. She'd entered it the moment she'd left his office, ensuring she could ignore his calls if needed.

But this wasn't a call; he'd sent a text.

Have ordered morning tea for staff. Please pick up the order from Le Miel on your way back.
Will be good to have staff bonding session.
Alex

Charlotte muttered an unsavoury curse under her breath and shoved her cell back in her pocket. She didn't need a staff bonding session. She'd already bonded with her boss and it had been so damn monumental she couldn't forget it.

Le Miel was a café they often used for work functions, and she figured he'd probably got the recommendation from the receptionist. Heading there would be good—she needed a friendly ear and Abby was a great listener. Though what her friend would say when she heard about the events of the last few days… Charlotte picked up the pace. The faster Abby talked sense into her, the better.

Ten minutes later, she had two bags filled with Abby's delectable pastries ready to take back to the office. But she couldn't leave without talking to her friend so she perched at her favourite table, ordered a cappuccino and waited.

Abby always popped out from the kitchen when she visited, which was several times a week. Charlotte couldn't resist her friend's melt-in-the-mouth *beignets*, croissants and *pain au chocolat*, eternally grateful for her fast metabolism that ensured a thirty-minute walk a day burned off the calories.

That leather bustier yesterday had been tighter than her usual size—a moderate B cup—so maybe she should lay off… She stopped eyeing up a giant almond croissant and sipped at her coffee instead, wishing she hadn't thought about that damn lingerie. She blamed it for her entire lapse in judgement. That, and Alex's inherent hotness.

Alex.

That was what he'd said to call him. Informal, casual, implying intimacy.

Hell, it was going to be a tough four weeks, waiting until the wunderkind yanked the accountancy firm out of the mire. It could only be a good thing, ensuring she had a job to support her impending loan. But four weeks of working alongside the guy who'd haunted her dreams last night would be torture.

'Hey, Char, what brings you by this time of day?' Abby collapsed into the chair opposite after placing a plate of freshly baked strawberry tartlets on the table between them. 'Your firm only ever orders afternoon tea and only then infrequently.'

'The new boss is trying to suck up to the employees.'

Abby smiled. 'So how is the boss from hell? Is he as intimidating in person as he was on the phone to you all these weeks?'

She'd whined about Alex for weeks—his condescending teasing, his constant demands, his infernal tasks—and Abby had been a sympathetic ear. Which would make what she had to divulge all the more shocking. Her friend would think she'd lost her mind.

'Uh... Alex is good.'

Abby's eyebrows shot up. 'That's interesting.'

'What?'

'You've never called him anything other than nasty names before. What's with the breathy tone? Is he hot?'

'You don't know the half of it,' Charlotte muttered, wishing she'd grabbed the morning tea order and made a run for it.

Abby grinned and rubbed her hands together. 'I sense a story.'

'Yeah, a horror story.' Charlotte sighed and internally debated how much to tell her friend.

'That bad, huh?' Abby patted her hand. 'Why don't you tell dear Abby all about it?'

Charlotte usually laughed at her friend's corny joke

whenever she used that line. She barely mustered a wan
smile today.

'I had sex with him.'

The tartlet Abby had halfway to her mouth fell to
the floor and landed upside down with a small splat.
'What did you just say?'

'You heard me.' Charlotte grimaced, hating the
way her stomach churned. She could have blamed it
on hunger, considering she hadn't eaten a thing since
last night, but she knew better. 'I did something crazy
yesterday and now the karma gods are paying me back
big time.'

Abby gaped at her and she didn't blame her. Charlotte hadn't had a date in all the time she'd known her
so the fact she'd just announced she'd had sex with her
boss would be as unbelievable as flying to the moon.

'I think you better start at the beginning.' Abby
grabbed a serviette, scooped up the smashed tartlet,
and placed it on the table. 'Though you'll have to make
it the quick version because I've got another batch of
croissants in the oven.'

Charlotte inhaled a breath and blew it out. Yeah,
like that would calm her nerves. Thinking about what
she'd done was bad enough. Articulating it would make
it all too real.

'Short version. My aunt got called away to Byron
Bay to help a sick friend. She had to urgently vacate
the warehouse she rents to store her merchandise and
asked me to do it. So I was there, packing stuff, when
the hottest guy on the planet walked in and we ended
up having sex.'

Jeez, it did sound crazier spoken out loud.

Abby, astute as ever, eyed her with speculation.

'You're not telling me everything. Why would you have sex with some random stranger, hot or otherwise?'

Heat flushed Charlotte's cheeks as she remembered exactly how hot sex with Alex had been. The way he'd looked at her, the way he'd touched her, the way he'd pounded into her…her insides clenched at the incredible, erotic memory. 'Well, I was in a weird mood, lamenting my rather pitiful social life, so decided to try on some of the lingerie.'

Abby let out a whoop of laughter. 'No way. He walked in on you?'

'In faux leather, no less. Bustier and thong. A real eye-opener.' Her sardonic response elicited more laughter.

'So you're blaming the lingerie?'

'If only.' Charlotte shook her head, wishing she could blame her lapse in judgement on something so trivial. 'The lingerie made me feel bold but it was more than that…he really *looked* at me and I liked it.'

'Oh, sweetie.' Abby leaned over and hugged her. 'You're beautiful. The guy has good taste.'

She snorted. 'I'm average at best and he must have thought I was easy in that get-up.'

Abby frowned and tut-tutted. 'Why do you put yourself down like that?'

'Habit,' Charlotte wanted to say, but she wisely kept silent. Abby had always chastised her for being self-pitying and Charlotte agreed it wasn't an attractive trait. Didn't mean it stopped her from lamenting her lack of a love life in her quieter moments.

'Anyway, I lost my head, had the best sex of my life, then walk into my new boss's office this morning and realise he's the hot-sex guy.'

'I can't believe this.' Abby's eyes widened, her expression awestruck. 'It's like something out of those romance novels you devour.'

'I know, right?' Charlotte couldn't help but smirk. 'Who knew I had an inner vixen?'

Abby squared her shoulders, her nod emphatic. 'Well, I think it's great. About time you had some fun.'

'It's not going to happen again.'

Despite that tiny, insistent voice deep inside that whispered how great it would be to feel that good again.

'How did he react when he saw you this morning?'

'Not surprised.'

Abby startled. 'You mean he knew? About you working for him?'

Charlotte nodded, anger quashing her momentarily lapse into wistful. 'Yeah. He's good at his job. Has a mega reputation in the accountancy world for taking ailing firms and turning them around. So he researched me. In his defence, he said he didn't recognise me—'

'I bet he didn't,' Abby chortled.

'I'd taken my hair down and my glasses off before trying on the lingerie, trying to get into some vampy character to see if I'd feel any different, so I guess I didn't look anything like my work picture.' She dabbed at pastry crumbs with her fingertip, pushing them around the plate, embarrassed to admit how she'd been role playing for a brief moment in time at that warehouse. 'He said he only recognised me later, when I used a phrase I've been using a lot in our business dealings.'

'Well, I'm assuming it wasn't *take me now*?'

Charlotte shot Abby a death glare and she laughed.

'He sounds like a bad, bad boy, not telling you the truth immediately when he recognised you.' Abby snapped her fingers. 'Hey, isn't that what you said you wanted before Mak left, a bad boy?'

'Yeah, be careful what you wish for.' Charlotte rolled her eyes. 'Now I have to work with that bad boy for a month and pretend he didn't rock my world. Several times.'

Abby beamed. 'You go, girl.'

Charlotte managed a wry smile. 'The only place I'm going right now is back to work with some of your amazing pastries, so the ratfink can try and buy us off with treats.'

Abby's smile faded. 'You'll be okay, yeah? Working with him?'

'I'll be fine,' Charlotte said, hoping her conviction lasted when faced with the prospect of working one-on-one with her dishy boss for the foreseeable future.

CHAPTER EIGHT

ALEX FOUND HIS gaze drifting to the elevator all too often as he mingled with staff in their cubicles. Charlotte should have been back by now and the longer she stayed away, the more he wondered whether she had done a runner.

Not that she struck him as the flighty type. Not if her work record was any indication. But if she'd been half as rattled as him after their earlier meeting...

Damn, he hadn't expected to be so affected by her. He'd been prepared to make his confession, ensure she understood and move on to work. He hadn't expected to be so confused.

His visceral reaction to seeing her again startled him. His gut had griped like he'd drunk too much fine cab sav when he'd seen her in that professional get-up. There'd been nothing remotely sexy about her skirt, blouse and jacket, but when she'd looked at him—albeit in stunned horror—he'd felt it like a kick in the head.

It had something to do with her eyes. Those cool, grey orbs held a world of secrets and he'd love to discover each and every one.

Yeah, like that was going to happen.

Alex had a job to do. Turn this company around. And Charlotte was a big part of making that happen.

As if thoughts of her had conjured her up, the elevator doors slid open and she stepped out, laden bags in each hand. The staff clearly looked forward to Le Miel's delights because they flocked to her, quickly taking the bags and heading for the mini conference room where they'd set up cutlery and crockery.

Her gaze homed in on him like a radar and he felt that kick again. It unsettled him and he reacted with a goofy grin. It didn't go over well if her raised eyebrow and supercilious expression were any indication.

He crossed the office, determined to set her at ease. They had a lot of work to do. 'Thanks for picking up the morning tea.' He gestured towards the conference room. 'Shall we?'

She didn't respond, other than a curt nod. He much preferred the warm, willing woman he'd held in his arms yesterday but knew her frosty counterpart would be much more conducive to work.

He followed her into the conference room, not surprised when she kept her distance. He chatted with staff, made small talk, discovering that Edgar had worked here the longest, an impressive twenty-four years, that Suzie had five kids, that Viola would happily take a redundancy to go farm alpacas and that Charlotte was the glue that held everyone together.

Staff raved about her, vindicating his choice to make her the new manager. She had smarts, kindness and respect, three traits that would ensure she excelled in the job.

But appointing her in that role meant they'd be working a lot closer together for his time here. The old manager had been responsible for running the place into the ground almost single-handedly and a lot of work had to be done to ensure it prospered again. He was up for the challenge. Would Charlotte be?

If she could barely stand to be in the same room as him, he doubted it.

As some of the workers drifted back to their cubicles, she finally approached him. 'You did a good thing with this morning tea, thanks.'

'Good working relations are important to me.'

Her eyes widened imperceptibly, pinning him with what he'd quickly come to recognise as her signature scepticism.

He hadn't meant it as anything other than what it was: a declaration to foster a solid work ethic. But she glared at him as if he'd made some gross sexual innuendo.

'We need to talk,' he said, making a grand show of glancing at his watch. 'You're a team leader here and I need to pick your brains about some of the ideas I've been kicking around.'

'Sure.' Her brisk nod was as terse as her response. 'I've got clients all afternoon so does first thing in the morning suit?'

Usually, he'd insist they work through dinner but in this case he'd be better off keeping his distance for now.

'Fine, see you at nine.'

She stared at him a second too long, as if she couldn't quite figure him out. That made two of them. Because as Charlotte stalked out of the conference room, he couldn't tear his gaze off her ass, the memory of how it had felt in his hands making his palms tingle.

After all his self-talk, he still wanted her.

Not good.

The smart thing to do would be to lock himself away in his office for the rest of the day, but that plan was shot to shit when he reviewed the latest performance reviews.

Staff cuts would have to be made if certain sectors of the company didn't start shouldering their load.

Which meant he had to play hardball.

He called the staff back into the conference at one and made his usual speech when he arrived at companies like this one.

'Thanks for taking a few minutes out of your busy day.' He pointed at the empty conference table. 'Sorry I didn't have time to organise a banquet lunch too.'

A few titters echoed through the group and he continued. 'As you know, I'm here to ensure The Number Makers becomes a viable company moving forward and the go-to accountancy firm in Sydney's eastern suburbs. To do that, the profit margins need to improve alongside work productivity.'

He paused, letting the implication sink in. He heard the sharp intake of breaths, the furtive glances, the stricken expressions. This part of his job sucked.

'I'm still in the process of reviewing all personnel's billable hours but I won't sugar-coat this. Cuts may need to be made.'

A paper clip bouncing off the carpet could have been heard at that point, the silence was that profound.

'Rest assured, that will be my last resort, but I wanted to be upfront with you on the first day so we all know where we stand.'

Feeling like an ogre trampling Lilliputians, he tried

his best reassuring smile. By the number of round eyes fixed on him, it didn't work.

'I'll be moving forward with a plan of action over the next week. In the meantime, keep up the good work.'

Damn, that sounded trite and condescending, considering he'd virtually threatened some of their jobs. He'd avoided making eye contact with Charlotte during his little speech but as the staff trickled out of the room, he couldn't resist.

Her reaction surprised him. That gleam in her eyes almost looked like admiration, before she turned her back and followed her co-workers out.

It gave him hope. Maybe this could work out after all.

If only he could stop staring at her cute ass.

CHAPTER NINE

WHEN ALEX HAD called the staff into the conference room at lunchtime, Charlotte had expected a pep talk.

She'd been impressed by his team-bonding exercise at morning tea and hadn't been afraid to tell him. It boded well that they'd resorted to polite indifference. She could do this. Work alongside him. Without constantly thinking about how damn incredible he'd felt inside her.

Yikes. That was the fifth time this afternoon she'd let her mind slip back to yesterday. She blamed him. If he didn't keep strutting around the office looking delectable in a navy suit, pale blue shirt and trendy stripy tie, she wouldn't be reminded of how hard his muscles had felt beneath that suit when she'd hung on for the ride of her life.

'Not helping,' she muttered as she prepared for the last client of the day. A call-up that she usually would have postponed until tomorrow considering she'd officially clocked off thirty minutes ago.

But with Alex's less than encouraging speech ringing in her ears, she needed to prove her indispensability and what better way than working late?

Her co-workers had skedaddled at five, either too

intimidated by Alex's threatening speech or too stupid to care. Whatever their reasoning, it didn't affect her. She had a job to do: to prove to the boss she'd inadvertently shagged that she'd become essential to taking the company forward.

Hopefully, taking on an unexpected client and working late would go some way to convincing him she'd do whatever it took to consolidate her position.

She also had an ulterior motive. If she impressed him with her work and appeared keen to toe his new company line, it would show him she'd forgotten their encounter. That it meant little in the grand scheme of their working relationship.

Utter bollocks, but it was her excuse and she was sticking to it.

Her new client turned out to be an ex-rugby league player who needed a new accountant to manage his business interests, a string of lucrative pubs. He dwarfed her office with his height and broad shoulders, which she couldn't help but notice in the vest top he wore, with shorts that accentuated well-toned legs.

In the past she'd surreptitiously ogle a guy like this, lamenting the fact he'd never notice a girl like her beyond her mathematical skills. But today, something had changed. The client openly flirted with her—and she enjoyed it.

Maybe the wild sex she'd had with Alex had given her a much-needed confidence boost, maybe wearing sensuous satin underwear for the first time made her meet the guy's eye when she'd usually look away. Whatever it was, she liked feeling this empowered. It boded well for chasing her dream.

'You've done a great job with keeping accurate records.' She turned the computer screen towards him. 'This is the program we use so whatever you need, don't hesitate to get in touch.'

His wolfish smile revealed a row of startlingly white teeth. 'Does that include calling you after hours?'

Her inner vixen did a little shimmy that he'd be remotely interested in her 'after hours'.

Her inner accountant shut down that vapid vixen quick smart.

'I'm available to answer your accountancy questions from nine 'til five.'

'Pity,' he said, his grin widening. 'If you ever fancy a drink, drop by one of my pubs and the staff will let me know you're around.'

'Thanks.' She stood to escort him to the door. 'But I don't mix business with pleasure. It's unprofessional and you wouldn't want someone like that handling your finances.'

He managed a rueful shrug while she hoped her nose wouldn't grow from telling that whopping great lie.

Because she had mixed business with pleasure, even if she hadn't known it at the time, and she couldn't stop thinking about it. Worse, how it might feel to do it again.

'I'll be in touch,' she said, waiting until the elevator doors had slid shut to toe off her shoes, pick them up and head to her office to pack up her things.

She'd almost reached her office when Alex's door flung open and she jumped. 'I thought you'd left with everyone else?'

'And leave you alone with that Neanderthal? Not bloody likely.' He almost growled, a deep frown marring his brow. 'You shouldn't smile at men like that. It gives them the wrong idea.'

'Excuse me?' The shoes fell from her fingers as outrage made her stand tall. 'My job is to make clients trust me enough to feel safe having me handle their money. That includes being polite. Which includes smiling.'

She flashed him her broadest, fakest smile. 'See? Nothing wrong with it. And while I understand you're the head honcho around here for the next month, I'd appreciate it if you would credit me with some business nous and butt the hell out.'

Probably not the smartest way to end her first day with the boss but he'd got her so damned riled she could barely see straight. God, the guy was insufferable. He'd reverted to the condescending know-it-all he'd been over the phone for the weeks they'd corresponded before actually meeting.

'In my office. Now,' he barked, turning his back on her and stalking into it.

Charlotte had two options. Flip him the bird, pick up her shoes and leave. Or do as he said so she could keep the job that was so important to her.

She chose the latter. But still flipped him the bird.

When she entered his office, he stepped around her and slammed the door shut.

'Just so you know, windows become reflective at night with the lights on in here,' he said, so close she could smell his distinctive aftershave, some expensive heady blend of citrus and spice. 'In case you ever needed to make rude signs at me in the future.'

Horrified, Charlotte felt heat scorch her cheeks. He'd seen her.

'Listen, we rub each other the wrong way—'

'Do we?' He spun around to face her, still so close

she could touch him if she were so inclined. 'I think the way we spark off each other has more to do with battling residual sexual tension.'

Damn, why did he say the S word? She could handle thinking about their encounter in her head, barely. Having him articulate it made it all too real. She needed to forget their sizzling connection, not remember.

'We agreed to forget about that,' she said, resorting to the same proper tone she'd used to put that rugby dude back in his place.

'We did and we will.' He glared at her, as if this buzz between them were all her fault. 'We're both professionals and I'm sure we can act like it.'

'Good,' she said, with a terse nod, but why didn't she believe him?

He sounded strained, as if articulating their need to keep things between them strictly business-focused was an effort.

'Maybe we should have dinner together? Clear the air, establish a better working rapport?'

'Dinner?' She made it sound like he'd invited her to eat rat poison with a side of nails.

The corners of his mouth twitched. 'You do eat, don't you?'

Yeah, but not with him. If keeping her mind on work in the office with him around was hard enough, trying to pretend she didn't want him over dinner would be impossible.

Sharing a meal implied camaraderie and intimacy, two things she couldn't associate with him. She had willpower; she wasn't a saint.

'I might have other plans.'

A blatant lie but it should let her off the hook.

To her surprise, anger darkened his eyes as he dragged a hand through his hair, appearing perplexed for the first time today. 'Don't tell me it's that rugby Neanderthal.'

Oh, my. Was that why he'd acted so crazy about her smiling at that client? Was he jealous?

No freaking way.

So she pushed him a little. 'Could be.'

His brows knitted together in a formidable frown. 'It's unprofessional to date clients.'

'And it's unprofessional to shag the boss but hey, we've already been there, done that, haven't we?'

She flashed a sickly sweet smile, silently berating herself for taunting him. A stupid, naive move when his gaze dropped to her mouth as if he envisaged the perfect way to shut her up.

Uh-oh.

'Alex, whatever you're thinking, you know this can't happen for a number of reasons. We just agreed to keep things professional because we're grown-ups. So get that look out of your eyes—'

'Damn it, I don't want to do this. I don't want to muddy our working relationship. But there's something about you…' He reached out, as if to touch her, before thinking better of it. 'I need to focus one hundred per cent on getting this company back on track and you're messing with that.'

He shook his head, his expression tortured. 'I can't get you out of my head and that lack of concentration is going to affect how I operate.'

His honesty impressed her and a small part of her couldn't help but be thrilled that a guy like him found a girl like her remotely memorable enough to distract.

'We can't,' she said, sounding less than convincing and they both knew it.

'You feel it too, don't you?' He took a step forward, invading her personal space, making her lean towards him inadvertently. 'Tell me you don't.'

Charlotte hated lies, but in that moment it was her only option. She opened her mouth but nothing came out. Instead, his gaze dropped to her lips again. Intense. Focused.

A second before he kissed her.

She should protest. She didn't. He had access to her mouth and he used it to wield his seductive power, the kind of power she'd never experienced before with any other man.

His tongue teased and taunted. Hot, long sweeps that demanded she match him. And she did, with more eagerness than she could have imagined.

His arms clamped around her waist and hauled her to him so she could feel every hard plane. And one very hard appendage.

She had to stop this before she lost her mind as well as her job. Her hands slid between them, her palms flat to his chest. She should shove him away. She didn't, enjoying the feel of his hard chest beneath her hands too much. Her fingers flexed slightly and he groaned into her mouth, his arms tightening in a vice-like grip.

He backed her towards the door, where he flicked the lock and hit a button that brought the blinds down over the windows.

Only when she nipped his bottom lip did he break the kiss, raising his head to stare at her in a daze.

She knew the feeling.

'I've wanted to do that all damn day,' he muttered,

his gaze dropping to her mouth again before returning
to her eyes. 'The way you kiss? Just as hot as yesterday.'

'Alex—'

'Fuck, even the way you say my name makes me
crazy.' He rested his forehead against hers, as if trying
to transfer his thoughts. If they were anything like hers,
three letters could sum them up: XXX.

'Do you want me as badly as I want you?' He lifted
his head and eyeballed her, daring her to disagree. 'I'll
be honest and say my work has suffered today because
I can't stop thinking about you.'

'Maybe you're just a crap boss?' she deadpanned,
biting her bottom lip to stop from laughing out loud at
his outraged expression.

'You'll pay for that,' he said, grinding his hips against
hers in a way that left little doubt as to the punishment
he had in mind. If that were the case, she'd be bad every
day. 'So what are we going to do?'

She knew what she wanted to do. Tear his clothes
off. Push him into the nearest chair. Straddle him. Ride
him until she could hardly walk.

But despite the sexy satin beneath her sedate clothes,
Charlotte was still the same shy, sensible woman she'd
always been. A woman who never broke rules. A
woman destined for a quiet, utilitarian life, the opposite of her parents.

She'd chosen to wear the frivolous underwear today
to see if the confidence garnered from yesterday would
continue. It looked like it had, but not in the way she'd
expected.

She'd wanted to impress her boss. Little did she know
she'd already done that by spreading her legs for him
yesterday.

She inwardly cringed. No matter what she wore beneath her clothes, no matter how much she got off on the power trip of feeling sexy yesterday, she couldn't change who she was. Not for this guy, not for any man.

So she said, 'I'm going back to my office, packing up my things and leaving.'

But she didn't move. She willed her legs to do something; they didn't respond. Her palms still splayed against his chest and his pelvis nestled against hers like they fitted. It felt good. Better than good. Having his body plastered to hers, her lips still tingling from his kiss, felt freaking fantastic.

For a girl who didn't feel this way very often—try never—it was difficult getting her head to work in sync with her heart.

She craved romance. Yearned for the buzz of electricity, the spark, that special something that ensured every day seemed brighter.

Once she'd got over the shock of her sexy stranger being her boss this morning, she had to admit she'd felt more alive. Secretly checking him out at morning tea. A pep in her step at lunch. Her stomach falling away when she'd seen his name pop up in her inbox.

Ludicrous. Ridiculous. Preposterous. The kind of dangerous reactions that could derail a woman's prudent plans.

Having him admit he felt this buzz between them too should make her happy. It didn't. Because as she stood in the circle of his arms, her heart still pounding, she'd never felt so confused.

She never threw caution to the wind. Never took a risk. Her parents did enough of that for all of them.

She weighed options, made calculated decisions. But

all she could think now, with him staring at her with open speculation, was that she had to take a gamble eventually and maybe she should bet on him.

'Do you really want to leave?' His hand drifted up to her face, cupped her cheek. 'Because if that's what you really want, I'll let you go and we'll never speak of this again. But after what just happened, despite all our protestations to keep things strictly professional, I think we might need to reassess.'

He was right, damn him. He might have bamboozled her but they had to get this sorted.

'I think we have good intentions to focus on work and we said all the right things, but that kiss...' Her hand drifted towards her mouth, her fingertips tracing where his lips had branded her. 'It's going to be tough. But I can't risk any fallout if we do something crazy like indulging in a...fling.'

Damn, even saying the word made her blush. She would never be the type of woman to indulge in a no-strings, brief affair, but having to work alongside Alex for the next month or so would sorely challenge her previous belief systems.

'What do you mean?'

'I need this job. A reliable, stable income is all important to me at this stage of my life and I can't let anything derail my plans.'

Crap, could she sound any more pompous? But she had to make him understand that while her body craved his, her mind couldn't be swayed.

'Does that mean you'd be up for a fling if we separated business from pleasure?'

She should have known he'd focus on that one word. *Fling.*

For her, it conjured visions of a confident woman making demands on a hot guy. Having him at her beck and call. Indulging secret fantasies. Being naughty and wanton.

And couldn't be further from her if she tried.

'I don't think I'm fling material,' she said, her voice embarrassingly wavering.

'You're an incredible, sensual woman who's making me go a little crazy.' He made loopy circles at his temple. 'We can call it a thing rather than a fling if that helps?'

She laughed, wishing he weren't so damn appealing.

He grinned back at her. 'If you're worried about us working together while we indulge this *thing* between us, don't be. I'm discreet. I can separate business from pleasure. And I plan on there being a lot of the latter if you come on this wild ride with me for the time I'm here.'

Four weeks. Twenty-eight days of hedonistic pleasure, the kind of which she only ever read and dreamed about. That was what Alex was promising her.

She'd never been so tempted.

But she couldn't shake her rational side. Indulging in a fling thing wasn't her style. Then again, no guy had been her style lately. Man drought would be an understatement.

'So this is a casual thing?' How she could sound so cool she had no idea, considering how loudly her blood pounded in her ears.

His eyes lit up, considering she'd acknowledged she might be interested. 'I'd never lead you on. I'm here for a month then I'll move to the next job. It's what I do. I hate being in one city, one town, for a long time. So yeah, it's casual.' He paused for emphasis. 'A monogamous casual fling thing, because I don't sleep around.'

His honesty blew her away. No man had spoken to her like this before. The guys she'd dated in university had been quiet, recalcitrant types as backward as her. They'd date a few times, end up in bed, with barely a spark. A bit of fun, a light-hearted distraction from the onerous study load.

None of those guys had lasted a month because she'd been a realist. Why waste time on someone that didn't do it for her?

Here was a guy, offering her a whirlwind, exciting four weeks and she was dithering.

Deep down she knew why.

She had her dream house in sight, which meant she had to go after the rest of her dream. The right guy. The kids. The dog. The herb garden. The veggie patch. The comfortable, steady life she'd always wanted.

And having a short-term fling, no matter how incredible the guy, and the sex, wasn't conducive to achieving it.

But she'd whined and moaned to her friends about this very thing, a lack of excitement in her life. Now she had six-three of hot male offering it to her on a platter and she couldn't say yes?

The pressure of his palm against her cheek increased slightly as his thumb brushed her bottom lip in an erotic sweep. 'No pressure, Charlie, this is entirely your decision, whatever you want to do.'

Damn, she must be in a bad way if him calling her Charlie sounded like an endearment rather than a taunt.

'I want…' *you*, she wanted to say. But the admission stuck in her throat.

So she quashed her rampant nerves, told her common sense to shut the hell up, broached the short distance between them, to show him what she wanted by slamming her mouth against his.

As her nerve endings fired to life again and he groaned into her mouth, she knew there was no turning back now.

CHAPTER TEN

ALEX HAD NEVER put himself out there like that with a woman before. Laying it all on the line before they started up.

Usually, he'd woo them a little, enjoy the sex, get to know them, see if a casual thing was worth pursuing. With Charlotte, he'd had the scintillating sex and bypassed the rest. And despite his initial misgivings that getting involved beyond work could pose a problem, he knew in his gut that this thing between them was worth pursuing.

He'd been impressed when she'd taken on a new client after hours and had decided to wait to speak to her. He hadn't expected to witness her morph into some kind of starstruck groupie around that rugby player. He'd seen guys like that before, had handled accounts for some of them. Big, beefy meatheads used to wielding their fame to get any woman they wanted then dumping them to move on to the next.

Alex had thought Charlie would cut the boof-head down to size. Instead, he'd watched her escort him into her office, then smile and chat as if they were old buddies, feeling the uncharacteristic stab of jealousy all the while.

It didn't make sense. He never got so involved with

any woman that he cared who they spoke to or how they did it, yet with Charlotte he'd found himself willing those damn elevator doors to close on the rugby player's ass so he could talk to her.

Her work ethic impressed him. The sex yesterday had blown his mind. But what did he really know about her beyond that?

He'd invited her into his office to talk. To show her that he was more than a guy who took advantage of a woman by fucking her. To get to know more about her in the hope of figuring out why she had such a hold on him when he barely knew her.

She wasn't his type. He preferred tall, leggy blondes. Charlie was a petite, slim brunette. Maybe that was the attraction? Opposites in every way? But he wasn't that shallow and knew it was more than that.

For the first time in a long time he found himself intrigued by a woman to the point that he couldn't get her out of his head.

So when she'd flipped him the bird, her defiance adding to her aura of mystery, he hadn't been able to resist her.

Worse, he'd found himself blurting out how much he wanted her and how long he wanted her for. Real smooth. Not.

He'd expected her to protest when he couldn't resist kissing her. He hadn't expected her whole-hearted response, let alone her agreeing to his terms.

What was it about this reserved woman that pushed his buttons in a major way?

She kissed him with unabashed enthusiasm, as if she couldn't get enough.

The feeling was entirely mutual.

Her hands slid down his chest, tentative at first. Skimming the waistband of his trousers. Sliding around his hips. Coming to rest on his ass, squeezing lightly.

He chuckled and eased away from her lips. 'Are you feeling me up?'

'Absolutely,' she said, her cheeks flushed, her eyes bright. 'Seeing as you so kindly explained how this thing between us will work, let me clue you in on how I see it working.'

God, he loved this feisty side of her, hidden beneath the pulled-back hair and the sedate clothes.

'Go ahead, fill me in.'

'You're absolutely right about keeping this a secret because if word got out I'd lose my credibility. And I want you to promise me that whatever happens in your revamp of this place, you'll only judge me on my work performance.'

He raised his hand in the way he'd seen countless witnesses do on courtroom TV dramas. 'Promise.'

'And before you go getting the wrong idea about me, yesterday was an aberration.'

Confused, he lowered his hand to rest it on her hip again. 'What do you mean?'

A deep crimson blush stained her cheeks. 'I don't wear raunchy lingerie. I don't have spontaneous sex. I don't do anything particularly adventurous, so if you think I'm some wanton sex goddess because of my crazy behaviour yesterday then you're wrong, and I don't want you getting the wrong idea because that lingerie was false advertising—'

'Whoa. Slow down. Take a breath.'

Could she be any more adorable? He knew she wasn't

the kind of woman to have a quickie with a stranger because of how delightfully flustered she'd been since. Even now, with her heightened colour and her bumbling rambles, she gave off an awkward vibe, as if she couldn't quite believe she couldn't resist him.

'I like you.' He hoped she accepted his intimate smile at face value, that he wasn't giving her some generic spiel to get into her panties again. 'I want to have fun with you while I'm in Sydney. No expectations.'

She took a long time to respond. 'But what if I disappoint you?'

She spoke so softly he wondered if he'd heard right. The woman who'd worn leather underwear yesterday and kissed him as if her life depended on it today must have some serious self-esteem issues to blurt something like that.

It saddened him, to think she didn't know exactly how amazing she was.

'Nothing about you could ever disappoint me,' he murmured, sliding his hands up her sides to rest on her shoulders. 'You're spectacular.'

'I'm average on a good day,' she responded drily, her lips quirked in a wry grin. 'But I can work it when I put my mind to it.'

He chuckled, loving her sense of humour. 'You know, I had every intention of ravaging you on my desk, right here, right now. But considering we already did the hot and steamy part yesterday, how about we backtrack a little and get to know each other?'

Her eyes widened until he could see the tiniest of green flecks amid all that grey. Like freshly mowed blades of grass against a slate path. Striking.

'Like a date, you mean?'

She sounded puzzled, as if she couldn't figure out why he'd want to spend time with her. Yeah, some prick must have dented her confidence real good. He could kill him for it.

'Yeah, if you want to call it that.'

A tiny furrow appeared between her brows. 'What do you want to call it?'

'Extended foreplay.' He winked, relieved to see her frown clearing. 'Trust me, sitting opposite you at some restaurant or café, sparring with you, wondering what you're wearing beneath your clothes, will make it all the sweeter when I get you naked later.'

Her breath whooshed out in a little exhalation as her colour deepened. 'Just so you know, I'm out of my depth here.'

'You don't date?'

'Rarely,' she muttered, her honesty surprising him again. 'But I like you.' The beguiling pink in her cheeks turned crimson. 'And I really like what we did yesterday. So yes, I'll go on a date with you.'

Alex had never met a woman so straightforward. The kind of women he dated were glamorous, confident and a tad whiny. They'd never articulate how much they'd enjoyed sex let alone admit they were insecure.

Charlotte was refreshing. His life might be ticking along just the way he wanted it, no roots in one place, constant travel, a healthy bank account, a stellar career, but he knew there'd been a certain repetitiveness to it lately.

Then he'd walked into that warehouse yesterday and boom! This woman had rocked his well-ordered life and hadn't stopped since.

'I haven't been to Sydney in a while. Do you want me

to get some recommendations for a restaurant or would you like to choose?' He wiggled his ass. 'I'm happy to be in your capable hands.'

As if she only just realised she still had his ass cheeks in her hands, she jumped and released him, making him chuckle. 'I prefer simple food over fancy.'

'Me too.'

She gnawed on her bottom lip for a moment, making him yearn to do the same. 'I love the freshness of Vietnamese food. Do you like it?'

'Love it.'

Frankly, he'd eat a plate of roasted cockroaches if it meant spending the evening getting to know her better.

'There's a little hole-in-the-wall café near my place. I practically live there.'

She tried to wriggle out of his grasp and he released her. But not before swooping in for another kiss. He liked her gasp of surprise, that he could catch her off guard. By the reserved front she presented he guessed that didn't happen very often.

She responded to him immediately, as she had earlier, open-mouthed, clutching at him, eager. Major turn on. Huge.

He wrenched his mouth away from hers before he reneged on his plan to take things slower after the fiery start they'd had.

'I'm hungry,' he said, tucking a strand of hair behind her ear. 'Vietnamese first.' He leaned in to whisper in her ear. 'You later.'

He heard the faintest of stifled moans and it shot straight to his straining cock. They had to get out of here. Now.

'Come on.' He grabbed her hand and opened the

door, studiously avoiding glancing at the desk and thinking how badly he wanted her spreadeagled on it.

That particular fantasy would have to wait for another day.

CHAPTER ELEVEN

CHARLOTTE HAD LOST her mind.

Giving into an impulse for sizzling sex with a stranger was one thing. Agreeing to have a short-term fling with him was another.

She'd been powerless under his onslaught of charm.

You're spectacular.

She was so far from spectacular it wasn't funny, but when Alex looked at her, he made her feel wanted in a way she'd never experienced.

He had this hold over her she couldn't explain. As if she could do anything and be anyone around him.

Maybe it was the transient nature of their liaison. Maybe it was the fact he was totally wrong for her. Whatever it was, she'd agreed to spend time with him for the next four weeks and she'd never felt so alive.

Even now, sitting across from him at her favourite Vietnamese restaurant, the place seemed less dingy and the prawn spring rolls more delicious.

'Do I have mint in my teeth?' He paused with a lettuce-wrapped spring roll halfway to his mouth. 'You're staring.'

'Just admiring the view.'

She shrugged, like it meant little being so open, when in fact she wasn't used to giving men compliments.

He smiled and she felt that same little hitch in her chest since she'd first laid eyes on him strolling into that back room at the warehouse. 'If you're trying to soften me up, you don't have to.' He crooked his finger and leaned forward, cupping his mouth to say in an exaggerated whisper, 'I'm definitely easy so you can have your wicked way with me later.'

She laughed, a loud burst that had her slapping her hand over her mouth.

'You've got a great laugh, don't stifle it.' He tilted his head, as if studying her. 'I may be pushing my luck here, considering you've already agreed to hang out with me for my time in Sydney. But I want you to make a concerted effort not to hold back with me, okay?'

He relaxed into his chair again. 'I like spontaneous.' His eyes fixed on her mouth, making her tingle all over. 'Like how you were yesterday, giving in to your first impulse. Go with that.'

She knew he wasn't just talking about the sex. But as long as she couched their fling in purely physical terms, she could protect her heart.

Because that was her greatest fear in agreeing to be reckless. That he'd walk away without looking back, just as he'd stipulated, while she'd be left nursing a slightly broken heart because she'd been dumb enough to fall for him despite trying otherwise.

'I'm not that person,' she said, mortification making her voice wobble a tad. 'I carefully consider options and make calculated decisions. It's what makes me a good accountant. But socially...' She grimaced. 'I'm awkward. Guys know it. Which is why I've never had a long-term boyfriend and haven't dated since uni.'

His mouth dropped open and the spring roll in his fingers plopped onto his plate. 'Never?'

She bit her bottom lip and shook her head, embarrassment making her want to slink under the table. 'I finished uni three years ago. Since then I've been establishing myself professionally and working towards buying my own home.'

She held up her thumb and forefinger an inch apart. 'I'm this close to achieving my goal. I've found my dream house. So I guess working hard doesn't leave much time for dating.'

He looked at her with a blatant scepticism she found disarming. 'You finish work at five. That leaves plenty of time to date.'

Charlotte wished she'd never started this. There was honesty and there was revealing too much. She'd done the latter. Now she'd have to tell him the rest, every mortifying moment.

'I prefer fictional men to the real thing. They don't disappoint.'

The corners of his mouth quirked. 'Care to tell me why I'm the exception?'

Her infernal blush returned, probably making her cheeks glow an alarming fire-engine red. 'You'll laugh.'

He held up his hand. 'Promise I won't.'

She'd come this far, she had nothing to lose in telling him all of it. Besides, she couldn't embarrass herself more than she already had. 'I'm close to putting a deposit down on my dream house. Which means I can follow through with the rest of my plans.'

'Go on.'

'I don't want to live in the house alone. I want a husband. Kids. The works.' She sighed at how embarrass-

ingly corny it sounded articulated out loud to a man
of the world like Alex. 'The kind of family life I never
had.'

His eyebrows rose. 'Your parents are dead?'

They might as well be for all the time she'd spent
with them growing up. They'd missed her first day at
school, countless award presentations, the day she made
the softball team, her graduation. She'd never forgiven
them for it.

'They're teachers for an international welfare organisa-
tion. I got dumped on my aunt Dee from the time I could
walk and talk. Well, not that early, but they left when I
turned six. They've flown in to Sydney on a whim a few
times over the years, never announcing their arrival and
they fly out again just as fast. Other people's kids are
more important to them than their own.'

He quickly masked his initial appalled reaction.
'You're their only kid?'

She nodded, bitterness making her nudge her plate
away. 'Aunt Dee is amazing. She's quirky and fun and
loving. She raised me, and I consider her more my mum
than my biological mother.'

Pity darkened his eyes. 'She's the one who runs the
online business that rented space in my warehouse?'

'That's the one.'

His lips eased into a full-blown smile. 'I have to meet
her, if only to thank her for giving her niece excellent
taste in lingerie.'

She gave him a look. 'You know I don't wear that
stuff all the time.'

'Actually, I don't.' He lowered his voice and it rippled
across her as if he'd caressed her skin with his finger-

tips. 'But I intend to find out, every single day for the next month.'

The bitterness clogging her throat evaporated under the onslaught of his charm. 'You're definitely the bad boy I pegged you for.'

Realisation lit his eyes and he snapped his fingers. 'So that's why you agreed to this fling. The good girl wants a bad boy before she settles down.'

'Something like that.'

'In that case, honey…' He held out his wrists to her, as if ready for handcuffing. 'I'm all yours, do your worst.'

She loved his overt flirting, the easy way he made her smile. 'Keep eating, otherwise the main course will never arrive.'

While he did as he was told and she savoured the succulent prawns in their crispy pastry shells, she couldn't help but feel glad she'd told him everything.

Well, almost everything.

He'd find out the rest soon enough, when they made it back to her apartment for dessert.

And she wasn't thinking about Abby's delectable pastries in her fridge.

This fling could be just what she needed before settling down to the serious business of finding her dream man to go with the dream house.

As long as she didn't cast Alex in that role, she'd be fine.

She'd never be so foolish as to do anything like that.

CHAPTER TWELVE

MAYBE ALEX'S IDEA to have dinner before getting his hands on her had been a bad idea. He'd envisaged extended foreplay; he hadn't expected to want to simply...touch her.

Not in a sexual way, but when she'd started telling him all that stuff about her folks and her lack of experience with men, he'd wanted to bundle her into his arms and never let go.

And that wasn't him.

He could deal with fun and flirty. Dangerous and dirty.

Emotions, he steered clear of. They bred dependency and complications and contempt. He'd seen what they'd done to his dad and he lived with the fallout of that tragedy every frigging day. It drove him, that unrelenting desire not to end up like his father—depressed, suppressed, a shadow of his former self before he ultimately ended his life.

Growing dependent on one person for happiness was a fool's errand. He sure as hell was no fool.

Hearing Charlotte talk about her folks had reminded him of how long it had been since he'd visited his mum. He rarely returned home to the outback town in northern New South Wales that held nothing but bitter memories. But he flew her to whatever city he was working in once a year, out of obligation.

On those tension-fraught visits they made polite small talk like two strangers. Something he guessed they were, considering the yawning emotional gap between them since his dad's death.

They never spoke about him. Ever.

He'd tried. Once. After the funeral. She'd shut him down. And Alex had maintained the awkward status quo for the last eight years.

'Can I get you anything?' Charlotte propped in the doorway between her small kitchen and lounge room, where he'd taken a seat as instructed when they'd entered her flat.

The place was neat yet cosy. Minimalist furniture. Bright rugs. Overflowing bookshelves. The contrast encapsulating this intriguing woman perfectly.

'Yeah. You. Naked. Here.' He patted his lap, his grin lascivious.

He liked seeing her smile. She should do it more often, to alleviate those shadows that lurked behind the grey depths of her eyes.

Her honesty over dinner had surprised him. Telling him about her inexperience with men, her frugal dating history, her parents... He'd wanted to know more about her since their initial encounter. He guessed he'd got his wish.

But at what cost? Growing closer to Charlotte, a deepening of intimacy beyond sex, could only end in disaster. She'd virtually told him as such, in her revelation about her dream.

She almost had the house, then she wanted the man.

He could see it so clearly. Some clean-cut man in a respectable profession. Probably a teacher. A banker. Maybe another accountant. Moving into Charlotte's dream house, making perfect babies, to go with her perfect life.

She deserved her dream.

Then why did the thought of her settling for sedate when she hadn't really lived yet bug the hell out of him?

He could have settled. Had the life his parents had. Marriage, mortgage, a kid. But he'd seen what that life could turn into and he wanted no part of it.

Ever.

'I was asking if you wanted a drink. Or dessert?'

'Only if I can eat it off you.' He stood and stalked towards her, one thing on his mind to obliterate the mood that thinking about the past never failed to elicit.

'On that note, I have a surprise for you.' She pointed at the sofa. 'But you have to sit and promise not to move.'

'Not promising anything,' he said, but he did as she instructed, intrigued by this playful side of her.

'See those boxes?' She pointed to an open door leading to a bedroom, filled to overflowing with boxes. 'That's all the stuff I packed up yesterday and there might just be more things I can try on and model for you, if you're game?'

He made a strangled sound and flopped back on the sofa. 'Stop. You're killing me.'

She laughed, a soft provocative tinkle that had him eyeing her with newfound respect. 'I figure that I became this hot, confident woman wearing that lingerie, it can't hurt to try again, right?'

'You don't need any of that stuff,' he said, suddenly

serious amid their light-hearted banter. 'The way we sparked? That's all you, babe.'

She flushed, her smile coy. 'Thanks, but I need to do this for me, okay?'

He nodded. 'Okay. Should I give scores out of ten for these outfits?'

'Only if you want me to use those painful-looking clamps I spied yesterday around a certain part of your anatomy.'

He winced and she laughed again. 'Be back in a minute.'

While he spent his life on the road and adventure was his middle name, sexually he'd never been into the kinky stuff. Or half the apparatus he'd glimpsed at the warehouse yesterday. Give him an armful of warm, sexy woman and he was a happy man. About to get happier as Charlotte peeked around the door, her cheeks a fetching pink.

'I'm not so sure about this…' She trailed off, sucking her bottom lip in. 'Nice in theory but now that I'm wearing it, I'm still a chicken at heart.'

'You're not a coward.' He eyeballed her, hoping to convey with one look how attractive he found her, with or without the sexy lingerie. 'You're a strong, confident woman who's taking control of her sexuality and indulging in a little fun. Nothing scary about that.'

His words hit the mark as her head tilted up and she opened the door wider.

Leaving him gobsmacked.

If that faux-leather black number she'd worn yesterday had turned him on, this sheer red chiffon thing shot him into the stratosphere.

It looked like an extremely short nightie that ended

at the tops of her thighs, held up by the thinnest spa-
ghetti straps. It fell loosely from top to bottom, making
it shapeless. But the fact he could see straight through
it, revealing dips and curves, and some equally sexy
underwear, made him want to sit up and howl.

'Too much?'

She sounded uncertain and doubts clouded her eyes
again.

He had to show her exactly how incredible she was.

'You're exquisite,' he said, surging to his feet. He
had to get his hands on her. Now.

'Uh-uh.' She waggled her finger at him. 'You're just
looking for now.'

'Spoilsport,' he muttered, sinking back into his seat,
adjusting himself as he did so. 'If I'm only allowed to
look, how about you take off that bra?'

He expected her to refuse. When she didn't, flicking
the clasp in front, tugging her arms out of the loops,
and letting it fall to the floor, his hopes soared. This
shy woman had untapped depths of sensuality he had
every intention of exploring in minute detail.

'Wow.' He stared in reverence at her dark nipples
clearly visible through the see-through chiffon. Her
breasts were perky, the areola perfectly defined. He
wanted his mouth on them so desperately his cock
throbbed.

'If you like that…' She hooked her thumbs into the
elastic of her panties and pushed them down to her ankles, kicking them off in a cute move that would have
looked practised coming from any other woman.

She straightened, her arms hanging loosely by her
sides, her expression uncertain, as she let him look
his fill.

And he did. He stared at the neat thatch of hair at the apex of her thighs. At those tempting nipples. Finally he reached her face.

When she slowly raised an eyebrow, as if taunting him with a 'what are you waiting for?' he practically leapt off the couch and vaulted the coffee table to get to her.

'What about the rest of the fashion show?' She grinned, as if she knew exactly how much she turned him on.

'Sweetheart, we've got a month for you to show me every goddamn scrap of underwear in those boxes but, right now, I need you real bad.'

To prove it, he grabbed her wrists and held them overhead as he had her up against the doorjamb, her eyes wide pools of shimmering desire.

'You are so frigging sexy,' he murmured, a second before he claimed her mouth.

She tasted sweet and decadent, like the after-dinner mints they'd enjoyed at the restaurant, her soft moan of pleasure firing his libido into overdrive. As if it needed the help.

He slid his hands under the nightie, seeking her breasts. A soft handful. Perfect. He rolled her nipples between his thumbs and forefingers as he plundered her mouth, loving how she strained against him, eager, wanton.

Her pelvis ground against his cock and he slid one of his hands lower to find her wet and wanting.

He delved between her slick folds, found the hard nub and rubbed, toyed a little, teasing her with his fingers, savouring the incoherent sounds she made. She was so responsive, so damn ready for him that it made his cock ache to be inside her.

She made soft mewling sounds as her excitement built and he circled her clit faster, stunned by how fast she climbed towards climax. His fingers continued to toy with her, to delve, and when she came apart he swallowed her cry of release, needing to be inside her so badly his balls ached.

When her body softened, his lips eased off the pressure, their kiss growing softer, gentler.

'You make me feel so good,' she murmured, burying her face against his shoulder, making something inexplicable tighten in his chest.

He got that urge again, to wrap his arms around her and hold on. To protect her. To cherish her. Like a goddamn knight.

To distract from the bizarre feeling in his chest, he got down to business. Unzipped. Condom on. Palmed her ass and lifted her a tad higher for easier access. Then he slid into the hilt. It was tight, wet heaven, her glorious pussy clenching around him like it would never let go.

She nipped at his shoulder as he withdrew and thrust again. Over and over. Swirls of pleasure pooling in his lower back. Making his balls lift. His cock so damn hard he felt invincible.

Her soft pants spurred him on. She scored his back as he drove into her with the mindless intensity of a man hell-bent on reliving the mind-numbing release he craved.

'So, so good,' she whispered. 'Amazing.'

Then she bit his shoulder, hard, and he came with the force of a hurricane slamming into him, spinning him around, leaving him disorientated.

At some point his forehead had connected with the doorjamb and when he could muster the strength he lifted it to find himself staring into Charlotte's grey eyes glowing like molten pyrite.

He wanted to speak. To tell her how damn unusual it was for him to have this kind of physical connection with a woman so soon.

He liked sex. He'd had a lot of it since his late teens, when he'd lost his virginity to a farmer's daughter three years his senior on a hay bale at the back of a shearing shed.

Casual sex had never steered him wrong. So what was it about Charlotte that made him feel as if what they'd shared, twice now, went beyond fucking?

'You're something else, you know that, right?'

Lame, as far as compliments went, but it had the desired result when she beamed at him.

'So does that mean you're up for another fashion parade tomorrow night?'

He laughed and tightened his hold around her waist. 'Babe, give me thirty minutes and you can model the rest tonight.'

Her hand skimmed his chest to settle over his heart. 'Make it fifteen and you've got a deal.'

'Hot damn,' he muttered, brushing a kiss across her lips, wondering how she'd managed to shatter his focus in just over twenty-four hours.

Usually, when he started at a new company, he'd remain one hundred per cent focused on getting the job done. Since yesterday, when he'd strolled into that warehouse and seen this shy accountant in her raunchy get-up, his intentions to concentrate on work only had been blown to smithereens.

He needed to get back in the game, ensure The Number Makers became a viable proposition again.

But when Charlotte's hand drifted from his chest and slid lower in that quiet, determined way she had, he thought, *tomorrow. I'll regain focus tomorrow.*

CHAPTER THIRTEEN

CHARLOTTE OPENED HER eyes at six a.m. every morning without the aid of an alarm. She'd do five yoga stretches in bed, a few ab crunches to get the blood pumping then head for the shower.

But something felt different this morning as her eyes fluttered open. More light streamed through the blinds, streaking the ceiling with slashes of gold and sienna. She blinked several times, stretched. Only to encounter sore muscles. All over her body.

What had she been doing…in an instant it came flooding back. Dinner. The crimson lingerie. Alex.

Bracing for the uncharacteristic sight of having a man in her bed, she gathered her meagre courage and rolled her head to one side.

Nothing.

Alex had gone.

Disappointment swamped her, making her choke up. Stupid, considering she understood the terms of their arrangement but when he'd agreed to spend the night she'd envisaged all sorts of crazy scenarios, like waking up next to him, cuddling, kissing, more…followed by breakfast.

Annoyed by her sentimentality, she pressed her

fingertips to her eyes, took a few deep breaths then opened them.

To find Alex propped in the doorway, wearing nothing but a towel and a smile, holding a cup of coffee.

'Morning,' he said, sounding way too chipper as he crossed her small bedroom to place the coffee on the side table. 'You were sleeping so soundly I didn't want to wake you.'

She wouldn't have minded him waking her if he'd done it with his hands and tongue but she kept that gem to herself. Just over a day in this guy's company and she'd turned into a sex maniac. Then again, considering what Alex could do in the bedroom…or the doorway… or the warehouse…a girl could be forgiven for focusing on getting down and dirty.

'What time is it?' The aroma of rich coffee beans tempted her and she reached for the cup.

'Six-forty.'

'Crap, I'm going to be late.' She sipped too deeply and scalded her tongue. 'Ouch.'

'Slow down, I hear the boss is lenient.'

His lopsided grin made her want to say 'screw work and come back to bed' but he'd returned to the doorway and she didn't know what this meant.

Was he regretting staying the night?

Was he in a hurry to leave?

Was he second-guessing his decision to have a fling with her?

'Thanks for the coffee,' she said, blowing on the steaming liquid before taking a slower sip this time. 'I can't function without a caffeine hit in the morning.'

'Same here.' He gestured at the towel. 'Hope you don't mind, I had a shower.'

'No problem.' She cradled the mug, letting the warmth infuse her to stave off a sudden chill.

Not that there was anything inherently wrong with their casual conversation but their exchange held nothing of the ease they'd experienced last night. Even during dinner, when she'd revealed all that stuff about her folks and her penchant for stability, there hadn't been this stiltedness.

She didn't like feeling like this. She was awkward enough around people, especially men, without adding to it.

He cleared his throat. 'I'll see you at the office.'

A statement, not a question, as he swivelled and strode back to the bathroom, where he would no doubt put his clothes on before beating a hasty retreat.

The unexpected sting of tears annoyed her anew. What the hell had she expected? For them to go into the office together?

She'd been the one to stipulate a strict privacy policy if they decided to indulge in this mutual attraction. The last thing she needed was anyone at work getting a hint of anything improper going on between her and the boss, not when there was a possible promotion in the foreseeable future.

But she'd be lying to herself if she didn't admit to expecting...*more* from their first morning-after encounter.

If they were this wooden now, how much worse would things be in the office? Had she been a fool to even contemplate separating business from pleasure?

She could do it. Could he?

Drinking the rest of her coffee, she waited for him to leave. The bathroom door opened in two minutes, indicating his desire for a speedy escape.

He stopped in the bedroom doorway, wearing the same clothes as last night yet managing to look impossibly fresh and gorgeous.

She waited for him to speak, to say something to banish the unease hanging like a pall in the air.

After what seemed like an eternity, he gave her a brusque nod. 'See you later.'

She waited until she heard the front door close before slumping back onto the pillow and muttering some very unsavoury names under her breath.

Whether directed at him or her, she had no idea.

CHAPTER FOURTEEN

ALEX COULDN'T STAND people who brought their problems to work. He had a firm belief that what happened outside office doors should stay there, which was why he had more than a few qualms about indulging in a steamy affair with Charlotte and not letting it interfere with their working relationship.

What a crock.

On all counts.

Because he'd certainly brought his mood into work with him today. An unsettled, God-awful mood he hadn't been able to shake since he'd first opened his eyes this morning to find a sexy, slumbering Charlotte next to him, looking like an innocent angel he'd willingly corrupted.

He hadn't wanted to spend the night. He never did. Sex he could do. Intimacy, not so much. But he'd been so knackered after his first day at The Number Makers, not to mention two sensational bouts of post-dinner sex, that he'd dozed after their second time in her bed and slept right through.

Another first, not waking several times. He never had a good night's sleep. Probably because the phone call regarding his dad's death had come through at one

thirty-seven a.m. all those years ago and he'd slept fit-
fully ever since.

He hated the phone ringing at night, but had learned
to cope considering overseas business calls rarely happened during the day because of time zones. But the
harsh jangle grated on his nerves, never failing to cata-
pult him back to that night when he'd heard his mum's
tremulous voice imparting the devastating news.

He'd known things had been rough for his dad, had
witnessed his depression first-hand. The stifling atmo-
sphere in the house he'd grown up in was one of the
reasons he had escaped as soon as humanly possible.

But the moment his mum had articulated the doubts
surrounding the death, that it might have been suicide,
the guilt had set in.

Had he done enough when he'd been home? There
had always been a wedge between him and his dad, an
invisible barrier that had prevented them from getting
close. He'd blamed his dad for being deliberately dis-
tant and he'd used that as an excuse not to visit home
as often as he should after he'd left.

Which of course led to the inevitable questions:
would his dad be alive if he'd visited more often?

Alex had refused to let the guilt eat away at him,
but in the wee small hours, when he couldn't control
his subconscious, the guilt festered and manifested in
the form of soul-destroying nightmares that ensured
he rarely slept well.

But last night with Charlotte curled into him like an
affectionate kitten, he'd slumbered soundly. When he'd
woken, feeling more rested than he had in years, the
sight that had greeted him had taken his breath away.

Dark, natural lashes fanning her cheeks. Her lips

parted, emitting tiny puffs of air. And the sheet draped across her waist, leaving her breasts bare.

He'd looked his fill, even though it seemed voyeuristic with her fast asleep, but he couldn't help it. Something about her inherent innocence captivated him in a way he hadn't expected after their first sizzling encounter.

How could a reserved, introverted woman be so fiery and uninhibited in bed?

Even though he hadn't known her identity when he'd first entered that warehouse and seen her in that racy lingerie, something about her had captured his attention. He'd glimpsed a hint of vulnerability despite her bold outfit and that contrast had snagged his interest like nothing else.

Interestingly, his desire for her hadn't abated since. If anything, after last night, he wanted her even more and that was what had sent him running from her bed before she woke.

Because while he'd been staring at her like a perv he'd started feeling…stuff. The kind of scary, terrifying stuff that confused the hell out of him, considering he'd known this woman for a grand total of two days.

It didn't make sense. He didn't do touchy-feely. He never invested emotionally in any of his liaisons. Yet waking up next to Charlotte had him wondering what it would be like to do this more often.

He'd hoped a cold shower would clear his head. It hadn't. If anything, his heart had still pounded madly when he'd peeped in on her before making coffee. Perhaps what he'd needed was a caffeine shot to really wake up. If anything, that had been the beginning of his downward spiralling mood because all he'd been

able to think about as he'd propped against her kitchen
bench waiting for her machine to fire up was how for
the first time in for ever this sense of domesticity didn't
frighten him.

It had been enough to have him bolting out of her
apartment asap. She'd seen it too, his fear. Had stared
at him in blatant confusion when he'd handed her a
cup of coffee and that confusion had given way to hurt
when he'd retreated.

He didn't do morning-afters for a reason and having Charlotte look at him like he'd stabbed her in the
heart reinforced why.

He never should have stayed the night.

Waking up next to her, battling the urge to linger,
had discombobulated him ever since.

He'd avoided her for the last four hours, not wanting to inflict his mood on her further. Thankfully, he
had a shitload of work to get through so the employees
thought nothing of him being holed away. But the fact
he'd deliberately ignored Charlotte all morning after the
evening they'd shared didn't sit well with him.

He wanted to make it up to her without giving her
the wrong idea.

*What idea's that, dickhead? That you might actu-
ally like her?*

'Shut the fuck up,' he muttered, his inner voice not
doing him any favours.

Two days. He'd known her a grand total of forty-
eight hours—he didn't count the numerous phone calls
to discuss business over the last few weeks. Because
the Charlotte who'd sounded so uptight and prim on the
phone that he hadn't been able to resist teasing her was
nothing like the real woman in front of him.

In the flesh, Charlotte Baxter was something else.

With a frustrated growl, he opened the folder containing the first lot of staff performance reviews. While he liked the freedom of moving from one company to another and the challenge of making it viable again, he hated this part of his job.

Sitting across from long-time employees who weren't performing to the best of their abilities; seeing the fear in their eyes; dealing with their overt hostility.

He'd seen it all in his time, from new hires who'd told him to stick his job up his ass and walked out, to the desperate breadwinners who'd do anything to keep their job, to the old-timers who knew if they were sacked they wouldn't find new employment.

Doing performance reviews at The Number Makers wouldn't be any different and, in the mood he was in, this had the potential to go pear-shaped. He'd be better off leaving the reviews until later and focusing on something less fraught, like client referrals.

He stared at the phone, dithering over whether to call Charlotte. She could help. She could give him an insight into the current system beyond the obvious.

Another thing he'd learned in his travels: figures didn't always tell the whole story and he wanted to ensure he did this right.

With a resigned sigh, he picked up the phone and stabbed at her office number. If the old manager had her on speed dial he must have conferred with her regularly. Then again, considering the hatchet job he'd done, maybe not. If the old fool had relied on Charlotte more often the company wouldn't be ailing.

When she picked up and responded with a cool, 'Yes? Can I help you?' Alex wished he hadn't rung her. Hearing her voice served like a kick to the head, his instantaneous reaction making his chest twang and his fingers dug into the wood of the desk while he clutched the phone to his ear with the other hand.

'Are you busy?'

'Always.' Her clipped response catapulted him back to the many times over the weeks she'd sounded just as dismissive, as if he was an unwelcome intrusion.

'Could you spare fifteen minutes to help me with something?'

She hesitated, as if remembering the last time she'd entered his office, and not wanting a repeat performance.

'Sure,' she finally said, her tone demure yet aloof. 'I'll be there in five.'

'Thanks.'

He hung up and let out a long breath. His plan to keep business and pleasure separate was fast becoming blurred if his visceral reaction to hearing her voice was any indication.

Even her terse, sharp responses reminded him of last night and the breathy way she'd murmured his name as he'd plunged into her, the whispers of want as he'd teased her with his tongue, the soft pants as her excitement had escalated.

'Hell,' he muttered, focusing on the documents in front of him and seeing nothing. The figures swam before his eyes as all he could see was Charlotte sitting up in bed, sleep tousled and adorable, staring at him with expectation.

He didn't like expectations where women were concerned. For the simple fact he could never live up to them.

He'd outlined their arrangement so clearly, had been

adamant he'd stick to it. But he hadn't banked on Charlotte getting under his skin, and knowing he had to see her shortly to discuss work meant he had to get his act together. Pronto.

A knock sounded at his door and he called out, 'Come in,' putting his game face on. The one he hoped conveyed professionalism, not the one that showed his inner turmoil.

She opened the door and strode into his office, defiantly meeting his eyes as if she expected him to bring up last night.

As if he would.

However, as his gaze flicked over her, taking in the calf-length grey fitted skirt, pale blue blouse and plain black pumps, all he could wonder was what lingerie she wore under the sedate outfit.

Which took him straight back to last night, exactly what he didn't want.

'We've got a lot of ground to cover,' he said, sounding way too abrupt as he gestured at the seat opposite. 'I need your input on the client referral system.'

She quirked a brow, impressively imperious, as if his attitude didn't impress her one bit. 'Why should my opinion matter?'

'Cut the crap,' he barked, instantly regretting it when her eyes widened in shock. 'Sorry, that came out wrong. I'm grouchy because of these.'

He pointed to the paper stack in front of him. 'I hate doing appraisals. It's the worst part of my job, coming into a new company and making the hard decisions based on performance. So I'm leaving these until later and dealing with the easier stuff first.'

He picked up a folder he'd set to one side and waved

it at her. 'By the way, this is yours and in case you're wondering it's beyond reproach. I'm not surprised the old manager suggested I liaise with you over the last few weeks.'

His apology and subsequent explanation for his terseness meant little considering her rigid posture didn't soften one iota. The frostiness turning her eyes a glacial grey was a dead giveaway too.

'I know how proficient my work is. I do a damn good job for my clients.' Her nose tilted in the air slightly and for the first time this morning he felt like smiling. Her snootiness was beyond cute. 'But if you think you'll get my help on the appraisals too, I'm not a tattle-tale.'

'I'm not that unprofessional. I'd never put you in that position.' He placed her folder off to one side. 'Like I did with you, I won't take the manager's word for it. I'll observe staff, check their billable hours versus productivity. I set you tasks over the last few weeks, made you jump through proverbial hoops and you proved your worth. That's what I'll do with the other staff.'

He drummed his fingers against the stack of files in front of him. 'I've done my homework on each and every employee. I know their strengths and weaknesses. But not everything is obvious on paper and I want to see first-hand what they're capable of. But for now, can you offer insight into this referral system?'

The disapproval pursing her mouth vanished. 'Fine, what would you like to know?'

For the next thirty minutes, Alex worked through the files, gaining more insight into the client referral system than he'd hoped for. As he already knew from her previous work, Charlotte articulated her opinions clearly and used facts to back them up.

She didn't mince words or show a hint of sentimentality for the old system, which surprised him. She might be an astute businesswoman but he'd figured she had a soft core and would try to sway him towards keeping the old system.

Her objectivity would make her perfect managerial material, just as he'd suspected.

When he'd closed the last file, she stood. 'Is there anything else?'

'No, that'll be all, thanks.'

She turned on her heel and stalked towards the door as if she couldn't wait to escape. He didn't blame her. Keeping business and pleasure separate was one thing, treating her with palpable coldness another.

It wasn't her fault he was in a funk.

Well, it partially was, but he was the one with the intimacy issues. She could obviously handle their scorching after-hour activities while maintaining a cool politeness at work, no problems at all.

'Charlie,' he called out, wanting to say something, anything, to make this awkwardness better.

However, as she turned and stared at him, a master of the poker face, he couldn't come up with one, single thing to say to make any of this better.

So he settled for a lame, 'Thanks for your help,' which she acknowledged with a brief nod before barging out of his office and slamming the door.

Reinforcing a clearly delineated line between the pleasure they'd shared last night and the business of today.

He should be happy. He wanted it this way.

Then why did he feel like flinging a stapler through the window?

CHAPTER FIFTEEN

CHARLOTTE COULDN'T STAND being in the office for another moment so at the conclusion of her meeting with Alex she grabbed her bag and laptop, told Reception she'd be working offsite for the afternoon, and hightailed it out of there.

She ran the gamut of emotions as she headed for Le Miel. Annoyance. Anger. Hurt. Self-doubt. And back to anger again.

How could he treat her like that?

She could have handled indifference but his obvious coldness had her doubting the wisdom of letting this man into her life, albeit only on a physical level.

She'd felt it before he'd bolted from her apartment, had put it down to the usual morning-after awkwardness. Not that she'd had much personal experience of it but she'd been floundering before he'd appeared in her bedroom bearing coffee.

When he'd fled, she'd made a decision to keep her distance at work and had managed to avoid him all morning. She'd been almost relieved when he'd called her into his office to work, thinking it would give them both the opportunity to laugh off last night and get down to business.

She'd been wrong.

He'd been brusque to the point of rudeness and even though he'd apologised, it hadn't eased the hurt deep inside.

She hated feeling so fragile, her latent insecurities ready to flare with the slightest provocation. She knew where her lack of self-worth stemmed from and it didn't make it any easier to deal with. Being abandoned by her parents at a young age ensured she'd always felt not quite good enough.

What was it about her that made them choose poorer children worldwide over their own child?

She'd always been a model child, a quiet kid who did exactly as she was told, with an innate sense of righteousness that ensured she wanted her parents to be proud of her.

She remembered bringing home a certificate her fourth week at primary school, a pink cardboard star for neat handwriting, being friendly to other kids and staying back to clean up at lunchtime. She'd loved that star, had clutched it to her chest with pride, not caring that gold glitter had become embedded in her jumper. When she'd presented it to her folks after school, they'd smiled, ruffled her hair and returned to scanning websites for their next lost cause. They'd never noticed that the pin on the corkboard hadn't stuck and the star had tumbled behind their desk. They hadn't cared.

She should have known then that nothing she did would ever be good enough, that they'd leave her regardless and it had been almost a year to the day afterward that they'd left her with Dee.

She'd felt lacking ever since.

Unfortunately, her inbuilt insecurities affected all

aspects of her life. She didn't feel confident with men so she'd never had a boyfriend. She didn't feel like she belonged in the trendy world of fashion, cafés and clubs, so she'd never had girlfriends. Sure, she'd hung out with fellow nerds at school and uni, quiet, diligent types who preferred studying to partying, who caught up for the occasional coffee, who were happy to share books but not much else. Acquaintances more than friends, the type of girls happy to hang out but only if it involved study load.

She hadn't minded at the time, or so she'd told herself to banish the desolation that swept over her at the oddest of moments, making her solitary existence seem so hollow. It gave her time to focus on achieving her goals. It didn't fill the forlorn ache in her heart.

Mak and Abby had been her first real friends and that had only come about because Mak had been her flatmate and nobody said no to the exuberant, bubbly dancer. Mak had brought her out of her shell a tad and had introduced her to Abby, but while she valued their friendship, she still felt different from those girls. They were determined and bold and confident, three things she could never be no matter how hard she tried.

She always felt inherently lonely.

Being dumped by her folks ensured she retreated from everyone, knowing that if her own parents could leave her others could too. She couldn't depend on anyone. Even her exuberant aunt Dee, who'd smothered her with love and attention, couldn't shake her unswerving sense of self-preservation.

Depending on others could result in her being alone and devalued. Again.

Which was why Alex's callous treatment now rankled so damn much. During their sizzling encounters he'd made her feel assured and she already liked it too much to be good for her.

She should never have agreed to a fling.

For someone who weighed decisions carefully, she'd sure lost her mind a little the day she'd had sex with a stranger, then followed that up with a steamy night with the promise of more.

So she'd responded in kind in the face of his hostility. Answered his questions regarding the referral system. Showed no emotion. And envisaged strangling him with one of the whips she'd glimpsed in her aunt's paraphernalia a few days ago.

Stomping into Le Miel, she had a craving for the biggest croissant Abby could create and one of the patisserie's signature hot chocolates. The more sugar, the better. She needed sweetening up today.

She also needed her friend to talk some sense into her, though she knew deep down she was well past that. For the simple fact that even after the way he'd proved how he intended on keeping business separate from pleasure, she still wanted him.

Last night reinforced that.

She'd never, ever felt that way.

Strong, confident, empowered.

The kind of woman who could actually inspire passion in a man. A woman confident in her own skin. A woman capable of taking pleasure as well as giving it.

She'd never been so brazen. Touching him everywhere. Kissing his ticklish spots. Exploring the hard planes of his amazing body with her hands. Sex with Alex was an eye-opening experience and then some.

She could attribute her feistiness to the lingerie.

She knew better.

Alex made her feel that way. As if she could demand gratification and seek it, could fulfil her deepest desires and his.

She likened it to shedding some of her reservations and being reborn. Wobbly and uncertain at first, but gaining confidence with each mind-blowing encounter.

It felt fan-freaking-tastic.

Maybe she should be thanking him for being so cold today. It reinforced that they were one way in the bedroom, another out of it. Smart people who could keep their sensual life separate from real life.

And if she was completely honest with herself, it was the most exciting thing she'd ever done.

Considering her residual insecurities, having this fling would be good for her. She could get it out of her system and, when Alex left, focus on finding her for ever guy.

A sound plan. If she could only ignore the deep-seated niggle that sex with Alex might have ruined her for any other man.

'Idiot,' she muttered, plonking her bag onto a chair and her laptop on the table.

'Talking to yourself isn't a good sign, you know.' Sean, the young guy who waited tables in the afternoons, grinned. 'How've you been, Charlotte?'

'Good,' she said, the trite response sounding like the hollow lie it was. 'Is Abby around?'

He shook his head. 'She had to fill in for a pastry class at the local cooking school.'

She didn't know whether to be peeved or relieved. Talking to her logical friend always served to calm her when things threatened her equilibrium, but she'd already told Abby about her first encounter with Alex and didn't want to rehash the events of last night.

Because last night had been special.

Dinner at her favourite Vietnamese restaurant had been the extended foreplay he'd predicted and she'd barely tasted the sublime food when all she'd been able to think about was sampling him later.

And sample she had. It had been stupendous.

She wanted more.

But at what cost to her pride?

Could she really put up with his insufferable arrogance at work then melt in his arms at night?

Doubtful.

She wasn't that good an actress, despite her new-found vamp powers.

'What'll you have?'

Snapping back to the present, she said, 'The biggest almond croissant you've got and a mega-large hot chocolate chaser.'

'Done.' Sean beamed, his fresh-faced enthusiasm making her feel a hundred years old. 'Not many women eat as much as you do. It's cool.'

'I think I should be insulted.' She smiled at his horror-struck expression. 'I'm kidding. I like food.'

And was blessed with a fast metabolism. One of the few good things her parents had bestowed on her.

'Coming right up,' he said, beating a hasty retreat, and Charlotte settled in for a few hours of work.

Only to discover she'd left her client files at the office.

'This just gets better and better,' she mumbled, reaching for her cell.

She'd get the office junior to bring the files to her,

and send back an afternoon tea treat to the office in return. After leaving a message with Reception, she fired
up her laptop and made a start, only stopping to demol-
ish the melt-in-the-mouth croissant and slurp down her
hot chocolate.

The sugar rush instantly comforted and as she waited
for her files she wondered if Alex would call her tonight
and if so what her response would be.

Fight or flee?

She had no idea.

CHAPTER SIXTEEN

ALEX'S MOOD DIDN'T improve after Charlotte left his office. If anything, it worsened because all he could think about was her wounded expression and it killed him that he'd put it there.

He'd treated her with a coldness bordering on contempt and all because he couldn't get a grip on his out-of-control reaction around her.

The entire time she'd been sitting opposite him, so prim and reserved, he'd wanted to rip open her blouse and check out the bra beneath it.

He'd wanted her spreadeagled on his desk, her panties around her ankles, so he could feast on her.

He'd needed to be inside her so damn badly it hurt.

So he'd done the only thing possible to hide his rampant lust: be cool to the point of abruptness.

She'd noticed. He'd seen it in the disapproving purse of her lips. Lips that had explored almost every inch of his body last night.

'Fuck.' He thumped his desk. Like that would help.

He had to see her away from the office, make amends for his boorish behaviour. He'd be honest, tell her how rattled he'd been this morning to wake up next to her, that it wasn't in him to deal emotionally so he never spent the night and he'd reacted badly because of it.

They'd worked through lunch so maybe he could ask her out for a coffee. But his plan hit a snag when he discovered she'd left the office to work offsite for the afternoon; to escape him, no doubt. Not that he blamed her. He'd been a stupid bastard, the way he'd handled this entire situation.

However, his luck took a turn for the better when he happened to be at Reception when a call came through from Charlotte, asking for files to be brought to her.

She expected a junior to do the job.

He had other ideas.

'I've got a meeting in the city so I'll drop those files off,' he said, pleased that the receptionist didn't find it odd that the boss wanted to do such a menial task.

'She's at Le Miel.' The receptionist handed him a stack of files with an elastic band around them. 'Tell her that if she doesn't send back afternoon tea for the crew she won't get her files next time.'

Alex smiled. 'Shall do.'

He liked the camaraderie among the team here. After working at many companies he'd witnessed his fair share of backstabbing and undercutting but workers at The Number Makers seemed to have a surprising bond despite the uncertainty in this economic climate.

Not that he'd be around beyond a month but he valued loyalty and it went a long way to helping him make the tough decisions when the time came.

Battling Sydney's mid-afternoon stream of traffic, he made it to Le Miel in thirty minutes. He had no idea what Charlotte's ties were to the patisserie but from what he'd heard she frequented the place a lot.

As he strode towards the shop and saw a young hipster guy grinning at her with obvious fondness, he hoped that wasn't why.

An uncharacteristic stab of jealousy made him falter. Had his foolish behaviour driven her into the arms of another guy? An old boyfriend perhaps?

However, the closer he got he realised the hipster couldn't be older than late teens. Considering Charlotte had to be mid-twenties tops it wasn't completely out of the question that she'd hook up with a young guy.

But she'd told him she hadn't dated since university and he knew he was being an idiot, jumping to stupid conclusions when he should be barging in there and making up for his behaviour.

Knowing he couldn't afford to botch this up, he pushed the glass door and entered gastronomic heaven. The aromas hit him first. Cinnamon, sugar, vanilla, and for a startling moment he catapulted back to the past. He remembered running into the kitchen back home after school, the same smells making him salivate as his mum took a batch of freshly baked cookies out of the oven.

He'd perch on a stool at the island bench, where she'd have a glass of icy chocolate milk waiting for him, and get his wrist playfully slapped while trying to sneak the cookies before they'd cooled.

Those had been good times, when his dad had still been employed and his mum would ask him about his day and he'd regale her with funny stories, like the time a goat got into the classroom and ate his teacher's curriculum, or the time the principal chased the school bully all the way down to the dam and fell in.

She'd laugh so hard. One of the few times he'd see

his mum laugh, which was why he'd tried so hard, often inventing stories just so he could see her happy.

Because young Alex knew that once his dad entered a room all the happiness drained out of his mum. They'd seemed to sap each other of any form of lightness and it had spiralled downward until his dad hadn't been able to take it any more.

When he'd got the call about his dad's death, the first thing he'd wondered was if he could have done more. If he'd stayed around, would his dad have had more reason to live? They'd had so little in common and when his father had rebuffed his constant overtures to be mates, Alex had stopped trying. Alex loved sports, his dad had hated them. Alex liked hiking beyond the farm, his dad had stayed within its boundaries, rarely venturing outside.

Losing his job had changed his father and for someone already on a slippery slope into moroseness it had pushed him over the edge. Alex had eventually decided to leave his dad alone, counting down the days until he could flee the oppressive house. He'd escaped Rocky Plains as soon as he finished high school and his dad had died four years later.

He didn't want to think about how his parents had co-existed after he left. He didn't want to surmise that his absence had thrust his parents together more, that their obvious friction would have quadrupled and that had ultimately led to his dad's demise.

'Alex?'

He blinked at the sound of his name, disconcerted by his memories, to find Charlotte staring at him.

Her eyes narrowed. She wasn't pleased to see him. 'What are you doing here?'

'I brought your files,' he said, fishing them out of his briefcase and laying them on the table beside her laptop.

'Uh, thanks.' She stared at him as if he'd personally delivered a ticking time bomb. 'Don't you have more important things to do?'

'Considering how I screwed up this morning, nothing's as important as making things right with you.'

His honesty surprised her, her sharp intake of breath followed by a subtle wariness as she eased back into her chair. As if she was trying to put as much distance between them as humanly possible.

She pinned him with a direct stare. 'Are you talking about the way you ran out of my apartment or the way you treated me in your office?'

She didn't flinch away from the truth. He admired that.

'Both,' he said, grimacing. 'Though they're linked.'

'Let me guess. You're trying so hard to keep business and pleasure separate that you had to prove you could leave my bed in the morning and treat me like a lowly employee at the office.' Disgust underpinned her accusation and he didn't blame her.

He shook his head, her insight not surprising him. She had a way of homing in on the truth without sugar-coating it. It was refreshing, when most of the women he'd been involved with in the past were master game players who couldn't admit the truth if it bit them on the ass.

'It's more complicated than that.'

She waited, not saying a word, her scepticism palpable.

'I don't do sleepovers,' he blurted, folding his arms. Yeah, as if that would stop the insistent urge to reach for her every time he was around her. 'So when I woke next to you this morning, it unnerved me and I didn't handle it very well.'

To his relief, the corners of her mouth twitched. 'Sleepovers involve popcorn and ice cream and horror-movie marathons and pyjamas.' She schooled her expression into a faux innocence he found delightful. 'And we had none of those things, so technically it wasn't a sleepover.'

'God, do you know how badly I want you right now?' he murmured, curling his fingers into fists under his arms to stop from reaching for her. 'You're this beguiling contrast of aloof one second, teasing the next. It's driving me nuts. I can't think. I can't concentrate, for wanting you.'

'Stop doing that.' She jabbed a finger at him. 'You can't go from making me want to slug you for your arrogance to making me want to straddle your lap.'

He stifled a groan. 'And that's another thing that drives me crazy about you. How blunt you are. I like it. A lot.'

'So what are we going to do about it?' Her eyes darkened to pewter, her dilated pupils making him want to yank her onto his lap, other customers be damned. 'Because here's another dose of that bluntness you seem to like so much about me. I won't tolerate being your play thing in bed then being given the frosty treatment in the office. It's not doable.'

She waggled her finger at him and he wanted to capture it and suck it into his mouth. 'I understand we need to keep business and pleasure separate. Heck, I stipulated it. But there's a difference between being polite co-workers and the way you treated me this morning.'

'Agreed.' He glanced around, saw that no one seemed

to be the slightest bit interested in what they were doing, and snagged her hand. 'I hated how cold I was to you in the office this morning, especially as my mood had more to do with me not being man enough to face my fears. Forgive me?'

Her lips parted on a surprised O and he'd never wanted to kiss any woman as badly as he wanted to kiss her at that moment.

'What fears?'

'Babe, you have no idea.' He raised her hand to his mouth and brushed a soft kiss across the back of it. 'I don't do commitment. I don't do emotional connection. I don't stay in one place long enough to make those things happen—'

'Which is why you don't sleep over.' She snapped the fingers of her free hand, shooting him a shy glance. 'So you've never stayed over at a girl's place, ever?'

'Plenty of women, never girls,' he deadpanned, earning a whack on his arm.

She laughed and the rich sound of genuine amusement lightened his heart. He'd been worried coming here that he might have screwed things up between them beyond repair but he should have known she'd be as magnanimous in this as she was in the way she'd handled every onerous task he'd thrown her way over the last few weeks.

'So we're okay?' He squeezed her hand before releasing it. 'You'll still work your way through that lingerie box for me?'

'Only if you're lucky.' She winked, her playful side so at odds with the woman he'd assumed she'd be from their business dealings that he couldn't help but stare.

'For now, I need to get back to work and you need to take afternoon tea back to the office.'

'You can come back with me, now that you know I won't bite your head off?' He waggled his eyebrows suggestively. 'Or we can skive off work for the rest of the afternoon and do naughty things to each other in private?'

Colour stained her cheeks but he glimpsed the gleam of excitement in her eyes. 'I have a lot of work to do and there'll be less distractions around here.'

'Okay, suit yourself.' He shrugged. 'But just so you know, I'm always up for that naughty stuff, any time.'

She took a long time to answer and when she did, it was worth the wait.

'Later.'

That one word pepped up his mood considerably and he made it his goal to show her exactly how crazy she drove him *later*.

CHAPTER SEVENTEEN

TRUE TO HER WORD, Charlotte had ploughed through a stack of work that afternoon. She'd completed tax assessments on three client files, a monumental task considering the level of complication. It had served its purpose.

Keeping her mind off Alex.

And she'd done the same thing for the next few days, working offsite, immersed in client files, determined to impress with her work ethic—and keep her hands off him.

She'd been blown away that he'd shown up at Le Miel to apologise, even more so by his honesty. And secretly thrilled that he'd spent a night with her earlier in the week, a first for him.

She shouldn't read too much into it. He'd probably been tired and fallen into a deep sleep. But the fact he'd acknowledged it meant something to her; that despite all his protestations about being unable to connect emotionally, maybe a small part of him already had.

They'd made their agreement, so the fact he'd spent the night shouldn't be such a big deal, yet why did it feel as if it was?

It made her wonder. Had she sensed something that

day at the warehouse? That this guy could pleasure her in a way no man ever had? That for once she'd rather live a fantasy, no matter how brief, rather than read about it?

An outlandish, ludicrous supposition, especially as she only dealt with facts and figures on a daily basis. But even when she'd learned her sexy stranger's true identity, she hadn't shied away from him. She'd tried; he had too, with their initial conversation to keep things professional.

She guessed she should be grateful that they were both adult enough to confront their unrelenting attraction and do something about it without letting it interfere with work. Well, not much anyway. Because every time she completed a task, every moment she had between clients, her thoughts drifted to Alex and how badly she wanted him.

It defied logic, this constant yearning to have him. She'd gone from celibate to sex maniac in no time.

Thanks to Alex.

She wanted to show him how much she appreciated his honesty and his apology earlier that week.

And she knew just the way to do it.

However, she dithered for a full hour and a half after her naughty idea first struck. She headed home and cleaned counters in the kitchen, scrubbed the bath, even disinfected the toilet, her least favourite job on the planet. Doing the most menial of tasks couldn't dislodge her idea and she pondered it.

Doing something so outrageous as turning up at his workplace on a Friday night with seduction in mind... baffled her. How could she, the queen of low self-confidence, do something like that, let alone think it?

Seduction was for self-assured women who knew what they wanted and weren't afraid to grab it.

Isn't that you lately?

'Dumbass voice of reason,' she muttered, sifting through the lingerie box for the hundredth time.

Silk and satin slid between her fingers, soft and sensuous, as she imagined Alex experiencing the same tactile sensations if she wore this stuff and he touched her…

With a frustrated growl, mind made up, she snagged what she needed, had a quick shower and headed back to the office before she could change her mind.

With a new boss intent on making changes, a few people would have stayed back to work late but most would have left by seven-thirty.

Even if a few foolhardy souls remained, Alex's door had a lock.

She'd texted him before she left home on the pretext of a work discussion to ensure he'd be at the office. He'd responded with a flirty 'work or *work*?' She'd left him guessing, responding that she'd be there in fifteen minutes.

She'd made it in ten.

After swiping her card through security, she entered the office, to find all the lights dimmed and not a workaholic in sight.

Good.

She'd worn flip-flops, easier to slip off, and a white cotton dress she'd picked up for ten dollars many moons ago.

A dress with a zipper down the front.

She'd bought it on impulse, when Mak and Abby had been hassling her to go clubbing with them. But she'd got

the flu and hadn't been too sorry to miss out on yet another social occasion where she would have felt gauche.
So she'd never worn it, as it made her feel slightly vulnerable having that zipper on it. As if it could slide down
at any time and reveal more than she intended.

Tonight, that was exactly what she hoped for.

For someone who'd ignored her sexuality for so long,
she'd turned a little slutty. And was enjoying every minute of it, despite her usual self-doubts rearing their ugly
heads at inopportune moments.

She could see it so clearly: being in her fifties, still
living in her dream cottage that she hoped to put a down
payment on in a fortnight, her kids dropping around
for a visit, cooking up a storm, but still remembering
during the odd illicit moment how she'd turned into
a vixen for that brief period at twenty-five before she
settled down.

In her daydream she could envisage a husband too,
the perfect guy who'd come home at the end of the day
and slip his arms around her waist from behind while
he nuzzled her neck.

She'd turn, secure in the circle of his arms…to find
Alex staring at her with blatant lust.

Charlotte stumbled and slammed her palm against
the nearest desk for support.

Alex couldn't be her dream husband.

He wasn't husband material.

He'd made that perfectly clear.

Mentally chastising herself for mixing up her day-
dreams, she traversed the office on steadier legs. With
every step she shed shy Charlotte and morphed into her
new sexier self, the kind of woman not averse to wearing scandalous lingerie with the aim to seduce.

Alex had articulated a particular fantasy to her.

She had every intention of making it come true.

He hadn't closed the door completely and muted light spilled out through a crack. She paused on the threshold and took a few steadying breaths to quell her rampant nerves. Wearing racy lingerie and a zippered dress might be a confidence boost, but going through a full-on, office-based seduction was another thing entirely.

Her arms tingled, nerve endings firing, and she shook them out. Rolled her shoulders. Yeah, like that would loosen her up. She did a few calf raises and managed a rueful smile. She wasn't warming up for a Zumba class; she was intent on getting Alex warmed up.

Before her meagre bravado fled entirely, she pushed open the door. And her lungs seized.

Alex was sprawled across the sofa to the right of his desk, intently studying a financial report. His hair was ruffled, like he'd run his hand through it several times. He'd lost the tie and undone the top two buttons on his shirt, leaving a tantalising glimpse of bronzed chest. He'd rolled up his shirtsleeves too, revealing strong forearms.

She had a thing for good arms on guys. Arms capable of handling a woman. She didn't mind a broad chest and firm ass either.

She flushed from head to toe as she recalled exploring much of his body that night he stayed over. Trailing her fingertips over all that gorgeous tanned skin, skirting over ridges and dips, mesmerised by the sheer beauty of the man.

And he was. Absolutely beautiful. Not an adjective used to describe men usually, but in Alex's case it fitted.

He glanced up at that moment, caught sight of her and smiled, sending her pulse into overdrive. 'Hey.'

She cleared her throat and managed a sedate 'hey' right back at him, as she entered the office and closed the door.

His eyes widened imperceptibly as she flicked the lock.

'Are you here to take advantage of a hard-working man?'

'Something like that,' she said, crossing the room to his desk, where she proceeded to remove items and stack them on the floor in neat piles.

'What are you doing?'

'Spring cleaning.'

He laughed and when she risked a sideways glance at him, she knew he knew. Her hands shook as she carefully lifted the PC screen and placed it next to the other items.

Only when the desk was completely clear did she turn towards him and crook her finger. 'Come here.'

He stood so fast the file on the sofa tumbled to the floor and documents scattered. He didn't care. He advanced towards her, the intent in his gaze making her skin pebble.

'Nice dress,' he said, stopping two feet in front of her.

'You think?' She shrugged, as if his proximity didn't affect her in the slightest, when in fact her heart thudded and the crispness of his aftershave flooded her senses, making her heady.

'Yeah.' He reached out and toyed with the zipper tab. 'I like this.' He inched it down slowly, the rasp of metal sharp in the air heightening her anticipation. 'Easy access.'

'That was the whole idea.'

She met his gaze boldly, feeling as if she were having an out-of-body experience as he lowered it all the way and pushed the dress off her shoulders, leaving her standing in a sheer white lace teddy that revealed more than it hid.

'Fuck me,' he murmured, his gaze heated as it zeroed in on her rigid nipples.

She wanted to say 'I intend to' but some of her brazenness fled when he reached out and touched between her legs.

And discovered the teddy was crotchless.

'You are something else,' he said, a second before his mouth crushed hers.

There was nothing soft or seductive about his kiss. He plundered her mouth. Ravaged her. His tongue mimicking what she yearned for him to do lower. Long, hot, open-mouthed kisses that had her clawing at him, desperate to gain purchase before she slid in a boneless puddle to the floor.

His hands spanned her waist and hoisted her onto the desk. She gasped as her butt hit the cool wood and he nudged her knees apart, stepping between them.

'Do you have any idea how much time I've spent fantasising about this very thing since you entered this office early in the week?'

Buoyed by his blatant lust, she nodded. 'You told me that first night you wanted to ravage me on your desk, so here I am.'

He shook his head, as if in a daze. 'How did I get so lucky?'

She raised an eyebrow. 'You could get luckier?'

He didn't need the encouragement, as he eased her

down with one hand until she was propped on her elbows, watching him watch her.

He didn't break eye contact as he peeled the teddy from her crotch to her stomach, leaving her bare to him. He knelt, reverent, and placed his mouth to her.

Feasted on her. Licking and sucking. Nibbling and nipping. He lapped at her, his tongue an exquisite torture as desire made her tremble. When his teeth scraped across her clit, she whimpered. And when he sucked, her hips jolted off the desk.

He drove her wild with his mouth as she climbed fast and furiously towards an orgasm that ripped through her so hard she almost passed out.

Her eyes had drifted shut at some point and when her eyelids fluttered open Alex towered over her, poised between her legs, unzipped and sheathed, his gaze hungry and focused.

'Look at me,' he demanded, as he slid into her inch by glorious inch, slowly, languorously, as if he had all the time in the world to pleasure her.

She bit her lip at the exquisite pressure of him filling her so completely. Then he started moving. Slowly at first. Withdrawing with infinite patience. Thrusting in hard. Maintaining this steady pace with a determination that defied logic.

How could he be so controlled when all she wanted was for him to pound into her like their previous encounters?

'You're determined to drive me nuts, aren't you?' She writhed and arched her hips upward but he held them down.

'It'll be worth it, sweetheart.'

And damn him, he was right. Because this time her

orgasm built slowly. Tension made her muscles tighten and her spine buzz. Her skin rippled with sensation, as if a thousand butterflies were dancing across it.

She watched him, his jaw clenched, a vein pulsating at his temple, his gaze focused on her. Only her.

She eyeballed him, wondering if he knew how damn good he made her feel, and whatever he saw in her eyes drove him over the edge as he pounded into her so hard she half lifted off the desk. His fingers dug into her butt as he stiffened and groaned, her orgasm crashing over her a second later.

They hadn't broken eye contact and for several long moments they stared at each other in stunned silence. At least, that was how she felt. Stupefied. Caught up in some weird alternate universe where she shed her shyness and thought nothing of seducing a hot guy on his desk.

'Have you had dinner?'

Of all the things she expected him to say after their mind-blowing encounter, that wasn't it.

'No.'

'Me either.' His lopsided grin made her heart twinge in a way it shouldn't. 'I think I've worked up an appetite. Want to grab a bite?'

Charlotte should say no. She shouldn't get into a pattern of indulging in date-like behaviour whenever they had sex, because it could only lead to expectations. Expectations far removed from their clear-cut fling. Expectations that would result in her wanting things she shouldn't.

'Stop over-thinking this.' He reached forward and traced the faint frown line between her brows. 'I like hanging out with you. We have to eat. Let's do it together.'

'Okay.' She found herself agreeing all too quickly. So much for not fostering expectations. 'I might need to go home and change first.'

'Why?' His fingertips traced a line from her brow, down her cheek, along her jaw, to her neck. From there, his hand drifted lower, between her breasts, across her ribs, coming to rest on her stomach where the teddy lay ruched up. 'This way, I'll know exactly what you're wearing beneath that dress and I'll look forward to taking it all off you later.'

Her insides clenched at the thought of more as a slow, lascivious grin spread across his face. 'I think your body agrees with me.'

She blushed. Of course he'd felt that, considering they were still engaged below the waist. How could she do this, lie sprawled across a desk, having a post-coital chat, not in the least bit self-conscious? It defied belief how this man could befuddle her to the point she shed her inhibitions.

'If you want to eat, we'll have to get dressed,' she said, adding a pelvic wiggle for good measure.

'If you keep doing that, we're not going anywhere,' he said, but slid out of her and took care of business while she redressed.

As she slid the dress zipper up, she caught sight of her reflection in a glass cabinet behind the desk. That was when reality set in.

Did she really think she could pull this off, playing a vamp only interested in one thing?

Because every time they had sex, Charlotte knew a small part of her craved more. The way he made her feel

when he pleasured her...she had a sneaking suspicion
that no other man would come close. And if that were
the case, was she setting herself up for a major fall?

What if her dream guy didn't do it for her like Alex?

Spending more time with him would only reinforce
this, which meant she had to get away.

Now.

'Sorry, can't do dinner, have to go,' she blurted, making a run for the door.

'What the—?'

'See you tomorrow.' Her fingers fumbled the lock
for a second but then she twisted it, opened the door
and fled.

CHAPTER EIGHTEEN

ALEX HAD NO idea what the hell had just happened.

One second he was on a high after having amazing sex on his desk, the next he was watching Charlotte flee his office after reneging on their dinner plans.

'Hey, wait up,' he yelled, giving chase. Thankfully, he caught her just before the elevator doors slid shut by sticking his hand between them.

They slid open to reveal her staring at him wide-eyed, her lips compressed in a mutinous line.

'What happened back there?'

'Nothing. I just remembered I have stuff to do.' She shook her head, soft brown waves tumbling over her shoulders, making him want to bury his nose in it and inhale the fruity fragrance of her shampoo.

'Let me guess. Feed your cat.' He snapped his fingers, trying to turn down the sarcasm but more than a tad annoyed at her sudden urge to flee after what had just happened in his office. 'But you forget that I've been to your flat and you don't have a cat. So what's up?'

'Can't you just let this go?' Colour suffused her cheeks and she folded her arms across her chest. Like that could ever distract him from her perfect, pert breasts.

'No. It's not in my nature to give up.'

When the elevator doors started pinging because he had his arms braced against them, he said, 'I'm coming with you.'

She glared at him, frown lines crinkling her forehead. 'I want to be alone.'

'No, you don't. You want to mull over what just happened. Maybe you're freaked out by how powerful the connection is when we have sex?' He stepped into the elevator and patted his pocket to ensure he had his cell and car keys. 'Don't be. Sex is rarely that good and when it is, you have to embrace it.'

He shot her a cheery wink. 'I have.'

'That's because you didn't have a choice,' she snapped. 'I strutted into your office like some ho and practically stripped in front of you.'

Her confession seriously rattled him. Was mortification behind her abrupt turnaround? He knew her inexperience with men could be an issue but the way she'd responded to him so far had convinced him that she'd shed her inhibitions.

He had to slow this down. Had to show her that he liked her for more than her body. Which he obviously hadn't done a very good job of so far.

'You're overwhelmed, I get it, but don't ever think I see you as anything other than a strong woman willing to embrace her sexuality.'

Her mouth softened at his declaration and he continued. 'I like being with you. That's it. No hidden agenda. No ulterior motives. So how about we take this down a notch? Grab takeout and go somewhere that makes you comfortable?'

A refusal hovered on her lips. He could see it in

every rigid line of her body. So rather than waiting for a response, he stepped completely into the elevator and stabbed at the button for the ground floor.

'You don't need to answer, just give me directions,' he said, watching the lit numbers on the console count down. 'Anywhere you want.'

When she still didn't speak, he risked a glance at her. She slowly turned towards him, her expression solemn.

'I feel like a big, greasy hamburger with a side of fries.'

Trying not to let his elation show that she'd capitulated, he nodded. 'Sounds good.'

When they reached the ground floor and exited the building, her continuing silence didn't disarm him so much. Whatever thoughts were going through her head were enough to scare her into this funk so he'd bide his time, feed her, then try a different tack.

That was when it hit him.

He never put this much effort into wooing a woman.

Especially not when they'd already done the deed.

Enough of a thought to send him into a funk too. Maybe he should cut his losses and run while he still could? The thought of working alongside her for the next three weeks, being forced to pretend platonic was fine; keeping his hands off her was a big ask.

He couldn't do it. Not when every time he sat at his desk he'd be bombarded with memories of her splayed across it.

Damn, he'd never get that image out of his mind.

She'd surprised him by taking the initiative, by boldly entering his domain with the sole purpose of seducing. It had turned him on big time. As for that dress and teddy, he hoped he could convince her to try on every single one of those decadent items from her aunt's kinky online store.

Not tonight. Tonight, he had to convince her that a fling didn't necessarily equate with making her feel cheap, that he valued their connection.

He'd assumed he'd already demonstrated that by taking her out to dinner earlier in the week but he should have known that with her inexperience she'd revert to type and withdraw.

When they reached the basement car park he placed a hand in the small of her back and guided her towards the right. 'We'll take my car.'

That way, she couldn't drive off and ditch him.

Surprisingly, she didn't protest and waited until they'd reached his car, opened the door and slid onto the passenger seat before speaking. 'Thanks.'

'For what?'

'Putting up with my freak-out.'

He grinned. 'Gorgeous, that wasn't a freak-out. That was you floundering after having the best sex of your life with a master.'

Her eyebrows shot up and the corners of her mouth eased into a semi-smile as he'd intended. 'A master, huh?'

'You can call me sir.'

With that, he closed the passenger door on her grin, walked around the car and slid into the driver's seat. They lapsed into a comfortable silence as he headed for the nearest fast-food outlet and ordered big. When they had a paper bag of burgers and fries, along with chocolate milkshakes, between them, he finally asked, 'Where to now?'

'I'll direct you,' she said, pressing her hand to her

stomach. 'And I'm not averse to you speeding a little, because those smells are making me hungry.'

He had a constant appetite around her but it sure as hell wasn't for food.

'How far?'

'Ten minutes.'

Thankfully, it was less in the evening traffic and they soon pulled up in a deserted parking lot on a beachside cliff top, completely isolated by a ring of trees.

'What is this place?' He hadn't been to this part of Sydney before, a trendy suburb on the outskirts of the affluent east.

'Eat first, talk later,' she said, tearing open the first bag, snaffling a fry and stuffing it into her mouth. 'Mmm…good,' she murmured, throwing in an appreciative moan that shot straight to his dick.

He'd heard her moan like that before, usually when he was thrusting inside her, her head thrashing from side to side, as if teetering on the brink between pleasure and pain.

Damn, he needed to eat pronto before he hauled her into the back seat and had his wicked way with her again.

'I didn't pick you for the junk-food type.' He unwrapped a burger, took the top off and removed the pickles.

'About the only good thing my parents ever gave me was a fast metabolism.' She raised her hamburger in the air. 'So I can eat as many of these as I want and not get fat. My friends hate me.'

He wanted to delve further into that offhand comment about her folks but he didn't want her to clam up again, not when she'd only just started talking.

'You've got a rocking bod. I'm very appreciative,' he said before taking a bite out of the burger and wishing he were nibbling on her.

She mumbled something unintelligible but he glimpsed happiness in her eyes.

They demolished the burgers and fries in record time—he couldn't remember the last time he had fast food, and thought it must taste better because of her.

'Shall we partake of our beverages outside?' He did a funny little half-bow that had her smiling at his faux formality.

'Sure, I've got something to show you anyway.'

They fell into step beside each other, slurping at their milkshakes, as they ducked between an opening in the trees and crossed a grassy knoll with a gradual incline.

'So this is one of your favourite places, huh?'

'It will be when I make an offer very soon.'

Offer? They crested the knoll and came to a road, lined by modest houses on the opposite side.

'There. That one,' she said, pointing to a weather-board Californian bungalow two houses to the left. 'That's my dream house and I'm going to buy it.'

He heard the wistfulness in her voice, and the pride behind her declaration.

'Good for you.'

His response fell flat as she half turned towards him. 'You don't like it?'

'I didn't say that.'

He didn't have to, considering his less than enthusiastic response was far from complimentary.

He hated feeling this way, oddly uncomfortable, staring at the small house with its newly painted white boards and ecru-trimmed windows. A towering euca-

lyptus smack bang in the middle of the neat lawn, edged
by flowerbeds. Complete with a goddamn picket fence,
a ludicrous duck-egg blue rather than white.

But something about the thought of Charlotte living
out her dream here, without him, didn't sit well.

Not that he wanted to be part of anyone's long-term
dreams, but just a week into their hot fling he didn't
want to think about it ending.

'You asked to see my go-to place and this is it,' she
said, the hurt in her voice making him want to slap
himself upside the head. 'I've been coming here almost daily for the last four weeks because it makes me
feel good.'

He understood that. Airports made him feel that
way. Tangible proof of his transient life, just the way
he liked it.

He didn't like becoming connected to anything or
anyone for too long, because he'd seen first-hand how
that bred contempt and eventually led to the disintegra-
tion of anything good.

He wasn't fool enough to believe that all marriages
were like his folks', but being cut off emotionally had
become so ingrained for him that he wasn't interested in
trying to rectify it. Getting too attached, letting himself
feel, meant that when life got hard, as it inevitably did,
the fall would be all the harder. He was many things; a
masochist wasn't one of them.

'Isn't the Sydney housing market booming right
now?'

His unspoken question hung between them: if this
dream house was so damn good, why hadn't it sold
during that time?

'It is, but the owner's asking price is too high.' She

ditched her milkshake in the nearby trash and wrapped her arms around her middle, as if seeking comfort. 'I've spoken to the realtor and told him my bottom line. He thinks he can get the owner to budge a little. So in the meantime I pray every night that the place won't get sold out from under me.'

She sounded so forlorn he couldn't resist touching her, resting his hand lightly on her shoulder. She didn't shrug it off, a good sign considering the way he'd doused her enthusiasm.

'Your dream is my nightmare,' he said quietly, knowing he had to come clean if he was to have any chance of spending more time with her.

'You don't own a house?' She studied him with an intensity that unnerved.

He shook his head. 'Plenty of investment properties but not a house I call home.'

'That's sad.'

He bristled at her audible pity. 'I had a home, the one I grew up in, and it sucked. So I promised myself the day I finally escaped that claustrophobic house in a dead-end town, and all the crap it held, that I wouldn't put myself in that kind of situation again.'

She paused, as if searching for the right words, before finally responding. 'A house can be a base. A place to put down roots. Nothing more.'

'That's bullshit and we both know it.'

Wishing he'd never revealed so much, he ditched his milkshake too and thrust his hands into his pockets. 'You made some offhand comment about your folks before. And you told me they travel the world. So no prizes for guessing that's why you want a stable base so badly.'

He didn't feel bad homing in on her weak spot, if the way she frowned was any indication. 'We all want the opposite of what we had growing up. For me, that's freedom. For you, it's stability.'

He gestured at the bungalow. 'I'm happy for you chasing your dream, truly, I am. But I see a woman who's led a quiet life, probably deliberately to be the opposite of her parents, who's willing to settle too soon before she's really experienced half of what's out there.'

He threw his arms wide, knowing he'd said too much when she turned away, but not before he'd glimpsed a sheen in her eyes.

Crap. He'd made her cry.

To her credit, he saw her shoulders draw back and her spine straighten before she turned back to him. 'And what's out there, Alex? What's the big attraction with living out of a suitcase, moving from place to place, never having time to build strong friendships and a steady relationship?'

Feeling like an absolute prick for trampling all over her dream when she'd had the guts to open up to him about it, he said, 'I just don't want you missing out on fun before you settle down.'

When anger flared in her eyes, he rushed on, 'Don't get me wrong, investing in Sydney property is like taking out shares in a gold mine. But taking on a hefty mortgage at your age before you've travelled and done all that exciting stuff is huge and I don't want you missing out on all that.'

She tilted her head to one side, studying him, and he had an uncanny feeling she could see right through his bullshit.

Because the moment he'd articulated how he didn't

want her missing out on adventure, he'd envisaged her having those adventures with him.

An outlandish thought, so far from left-field it wasn't funny, but the moment it popped into his head he could see it so clearly. If she'd awakened sexually with him, what would it be like to show her more? To show her the world?

He didn't want stability but he wouldn't be averse to having a wondrous woman by his side on his travels.

Ridiculous. He'd known her a grand total of five weeks, four of those via telephone and email.

So why the hell was he contemplating something so bizarre?

Not to mention one salient point.

He'd earmarked her as the new manager for The Number Makers, a secure job that would ensure she could afford the dream house in front of him.

Managerial accountants didn't throw away their sensible dreams to follow a whim.

Shaking his head to clear it, he reached for her, relieved when she let him hold her hands. 'You know what? Forget everything I said. Maybe I'm a little jealous, seeing evidence of how much more evolved you are when I'm a thirty-two-year-old wanderer who will never settle down for anything.'

He must have finally said the right thing because the tension from her face drained away. 'You're jealous?'

She sounded incredulous, an improvement on the hurt, so he continued.

'I think so.' He squeezed her hands. 'At your age I was still partying hard while building my empire.'

The corners of her mouth quirked. 'You don't have an empire.'

He released one of her hands to tap his temple. 'Up here I do. And it's a magical place, filled with nubile women and endless dollars hanging from money trees and a dashing, handsome king who does what he wants when he wants.'

'That's some imagination.' Her wry smile lightened his heart. 'I guess we agree to disagree on what constitutes a future.'

'Yeah.' He tugged on her hand, drawing her close. 'And thank you for showing me your dream. I'm happy for you. And I'm sorry for raining all over it with my bluntness.'

'I like bluntness, just like you do,' she said, resting her head against his chest. 'We don't have much time together so why waste it pussyfooting around and playing games?'

As Alex slid his arms around her waist and hugged her tight, he got that feeling again. The one he'd had earlier when he'd thought of her living her dream life in this place. Like indigestion burning his gullet, only stronger.

'We don't have much time together.'

Usually, he'd be relieved she knew the score.

So what the hell was his problem?

CHAPTER NINETEEN

CHARLOTTE HAD TO get this relationship back onto familiar footing before she made a complete ass of herself.

She never should have brought him here.

What had she expected? That he'd take one look at her dream house after knowing her for five minutes and fall headlong into her happily-ever-after fantasy?

She was an idiot.

An idiot who now had to distract herself fast before she blubbered all over him.

So she did the one thing guaranteed to get this fling back on track.

Focus on sex.

'Come with me.' She grabbed his hand and tugged, half jogging back to the car.

He was only too happy to keep up with her, one of his long strides matching two of hers. This eagerness to pleasure each other was good. It kept her mind focused on the physical, not leaving her much room to dwell on the unanswered questions buzzing around her head like pesky flies.

What had happened in Alex's past to ensure he never wanted to put down roots? Why did he consider his childhood home and town claustrophobic? Who had caused such emotional damage that at thirty-two he refused to settle down?

And the doozy, why did he have to go and plant that seed of doubt, that maybe taking on a big mortgage before she'd done exciting stuff like travel was a mistake?

She had a goal. A dream. And nobody, especially some charming wanderer, would distract her from it.

She needed this house.

She needed a clear-cut plan for the future.

She didn't need to be swayed, no matter how tempting the momentary vision of freedom he'd planted in her head.

What would it be like to chuck in her job to go travelling for a year? To not worry about getting up to the annoying buzz of an alarm, to spend her days exploring new cities rather than stuck behind a desk using her mathematical skills, to meet new people and expand her social group?

For those few moments Alex had lectured her about his concern for her settling too soon, she'd envisioned a different life.

It could be wonderful.

It could also result in her ending up like her folks, with nothing to show for their years of work, and there was no way in hell she'd be inflicting that kind of life on her children.

They reached the car and she perched on the bonnet, the metal still warm beneath her butt. She took charge, grabbing his lapels and tugging him close, her kiss clumsy but effective as he groaned and nestled between her thighs, the material of his trousers rasping against her skin in a delicious chafe.

She decided then and there to frame this dress.

'Let's get inside the car,' he murmured, nipping her

earlobe before sucking it into his mouth and toying with it using his tongue.

She shivered at the sensation flooding her body and wrapped her legs around him in response. 'No. I like feeling this…exposed.'

He grinned, his teeth almost luminous in the moonlight. 'A risk-taker, huh?'

'Only with you,' she said, meaning it.

For a guy she hardly knew, Alex made her feel safe in a way she never would have thought possible.

It took her ages to warm up to people usually, which explained why she hardly had any friends.

Mak had been her flatmate, and so overtly exuberant and friendly that Charlotte had eventually had no choice but to let her into her heart. Abby had been Mak's friend, a co-worker initially, and it seemed inevitable that the three of them had started hanging out.

She missed Mak terribly, but didn't begrudge her friend chasing her dream to dance on Broadway. She missed Abby too, considering her job at Le Miel and her sexy man Tanner kept her too busy to hang out as often as they used to.

Maybe that was why she'd let Alex into her life so quickly? Loneliness. Then again, she'd been lonely for most of her life courtesy of her inherent insecurities, so maybe she was grasping at any excuse for her wanton brazenness when it came to this man?

'You're killing me, sweetheart.' He rested his forehead against hers. 'I don't have another condom on me.'

For a second she contemplated saying *screw it*, but her rational side wouldn't be denied. While she hadn't slept with anyone in years, a guy who looked like Alex who embraced a wandering lifestyle certainly wouldn't have been celibate.

'I'm clean, in case you were wondering,' he said, as if reading her mind, 'but I don't do unprotected sex.'

He hesitated, as if unsure whether to say more, before adding, 'I don't see kids in my future so I won't risk it.'

As if she needed another reminder of why they could never be anything other than a short-term fling. But knowing they could never be more than this and having it shoved down her throat were worlds apart.

She could have pointed out that condoms weren't fool-proof and considering she wasn't on a contraceptive—she'd need to have regular sex to consider it—they were playing Russian roulette every time they did the deed.

But this wasn't the moment to lecture. She needed to stop the questions pinging in her brain and sex with Alex was guaranteed to do that.

'We can do other stuff,' she said, with a coy toss of her head, a move she'd never tried in her life but which seemed to work as his gaze brightened.

'We could get arrested for public indecency by doing *other stuff* out here.'

She didn't want to explain that she came here every night to stare wistfully at her dream house and no one else ever did, so she unwound her legs and slid off the bonnet.

'There's always the back seat?' She raised an eyebrow in invitation and thankfully he didn't need to be asked twice.

'You're incredibly naughty,' he said, opening the door and waiting for her to scoot across the seat before joining her. 'I like it.'

He closed the door and activated the locks, his gaze

inscrutable in the darkness as clouds scudded across the moon. 'Lie back.' His command held a hint of desperation, like he couldn't wait to go down on her.

'No.'

She needed to be in control this time. She needed to prove to herself that she had a handle on this thing developing between them because, deep down, their connection was more than sex and they both knew it.

Scooting closer, she placed a hand over his zipper and the sizeable bulge beneath it.

His sharp intake of breath hissed out slowly as she eased the zipper down, the rasp of metal teeth unlocking the only sound in the car.

'Charlie…'

She had no idea if his warning growl meant stop or hurry up so she reached inside his jocks and wrapped her fingers around velvet steel.

'Fuck,' he muttered as she took him out and slid her hand up and down experimentally, getting a feel for what he liked by listening to the changes in his breathing.

When she brushed her thumb over the head he jerked slightly.

'You like that?' She did it again, savouring the power that came with making a man like Alex needy.

'I like everything you do to me,' he said through gritted teeth as she squeezed harder.

'Good,' she said, leaning forward to lick him.

His hips lifted off the seat slightly. She took it as a good sign.

She'd never done this before and while she had reservations about putting something so big in her mouth, she wanted to experience everything she could with this incredible man.

Tentatively she wrapped her lips around him. He tasted musky, almost sweet, and she lapped a little. He moaned again and rested his hand on her head, his fingers twining in her hair a little.

Emboldened, she took him deeper into her mouth, as far as she could without gagging, leaving her enough room to fit an entire hand around what was left over.

No surprise why he felt so damn good inside her.

She started to move, slowly at first. Sliding him out of her mouth and back in, her fist moving in synchronicity.

He liked it, if his low groans were any indication. She liked it too, liked lapping him, licking him. Her very own Popsicle. She almost giggled at the thought but didn't want to kill the mood. Or choke.

Besides, giving her first blowjob was having an unexpected effect on her. She'd never expected to be this turned on.

She shifted restlessly and, as if sensing her need, he leaned sideways and slipped a hand between her legs. It wasn't the most comfortable positioning, being squished into the back of a car, her knees on the floor with her head in his lap, him half draped along the backseat, one hand on the back of her head, the other doing wicked things between her legs, but they made it work.

As he zeroed in on her clit and rubbed it, she automatically picked up the pace, sucking harder as her head bobbed and her hand pumped.

His hand tightened on the back of her head, tugging painfully at her hair. She didn't care, as the pleasure built from his other hand's ministrations. Pushing her higher, faster, than ever before until she fell over the edge into blissful oblivion.

With a garbled cry he followed, the heat of him in her mouth like nothing she could have anticipated. It was so damn sexy.

After unkinking their bodies like a couple of contortionists, she sat next to him, content to rest her head in the crook of his shoulder.

'You're incredible,' he said, turning his head to brush a kiss across her forehead. 'And just full of surprises.'

'You ain't seen nothing yet.'

Her flippant response lost some of its impact when she ended on an embarrassing hiccup and he eased away, searching her face for some clue as to her emotional state.

Good luck with that, she thought, as she had no idea how the hell she'd ended up here, in the back seat of some hot guy's car, giving him head when she wanted to give him her heart.

But she couldn't and that ensured there'd be more focus on sex, less dwelling on things she couldn't have.

'What's wrong?'

He placed a finger under her chin and tilted her head up. Not that he'd be able to read much in the dim interior. She'd never been more grateful for clouds covering the moon in all her life.

'Nothing.'

'You know I'm going to keep pestering you until you tell me, right?'

Already feeling too fragile, she couldn't withstand an interrogation, so she settled for a half-truth.

'That's the first time I did *that* and I'm wondering if I was okay.'

She only just heard his muttered, 'What the fuck?' as he swivelled to face her completely.

'You mean…' He cleared his throat, more stunned than she'd expected. 'That was your first blowjob?'

'Uh-huh.' She shrugged, as if it meant little, when in fact she was more than a little curious to hear his evaluation.

Not that she wanted a score, per se, but a little feedback wouldn't hurt for future reference.

'Babe, what you did with your mouth and your hand…' He shook his head, as if trying to clear it. 'Phenomenal.'

She grinned like he'd presented her with a gold medal for fellatio. 'Really?'

'Really.' He grinned back at her and at that moment the clouds cleared the moon and she spied a glint in his eyes in the resulting light flooding the car. 'Though maybe I should lie and say you were average, which means you'd need to do a hell of a lot of practice?'

'I'm sure I could find willing subjects for that,' she deadpanned, unprepared for his hand to shoot out and tweak her nose.

She squealed and swatted him away, but they ended up mock wrestling and laughing and falling on top of each other.

'This is nice,' she said, when they finally drew apart to catch their breath.

'Us being in the back seat?'

'Us playing and swapping banter after sharing something intimate.' She laid a hand on his chest. 'I never expected to feel this comfortable about sex, especially after not knowing you that long, but I feel good being with you like this.'

'Feeling's mutual, sweetheart.'

He enveloped her in a squishy hug and while she knew his endearment didn't mean much, in that moment, in the circle of his arms, her heart squirming with neediness, she wished it did.

CHAPTER TWENTY

ALEX DROPPED CHARLOTTE back at her car at work, followed her home to ensure she got there safely, then slunk off into the night like a goddamn coward.

She'd asked him to stay.

He'd cited work.

Yep, a coward. A lily-livered, low-bellied coward who couldn't face seeing her any longer tonight in case he blurted the truth.

How seeing her dream house scared the shit out of him.

He'd acted like a real prick too, spouting all that crap about her settling down too soon before experiencing life. Then had to backtrack when he'd seen how badly he'd hurt her.

He should have taken her home then. Instead, he'd been the recipient of the best head of his life. She'd blown his mind, literally, yet while he'd been coming down from his high all he'd been able to think about was her in that damn house without him.

Or with him.

And that was what had him in such a funk he'd hightailed it away from her flat so fast his tyres had spun.

Because the moment she'd shown him that damn

Californian bungalow with its garish blue picket fence, he'd pictured her on the front step and him coming home to her. Or maybe the other way round.

She'd be a kickass manager when he promoted her so maybe he could stay home for a while and stop flitting. Whip up gourmet meals for his hard-working woman. Have an open bottle of red on the dining table waiting for her at the end of a long day. Be a supportive sounding-board. Draw her a bath…

He couldn't have any part of that.

When he reached his hotel in record time, he showered and dressed, slapped some aftershave on his cheeks and ran a comb through his hair.

He knew what he needed to get him out of this funk.

He needed to remind himself of why he chose this kind of life and how good it made him feel.

So he headed for the one place that could guarantee him a shot of reality anywhere in the world.

The hotel bar.

It didn't matter where he stayed in Australia or the UK or Asia, he always frequented the hotel bar. Not because he had a drinking problem but for the special brand of camaraderie that could only be found among fellow nomads.

People who loved to travel. People who had wander-lust in their veins. People who valued adventure over stability.

Right now, he needed to be with his people.

Entering the bar, he headed for a vacant stool smack bang in the middle of the trendy stainless-steel bar running the length of the room. His vantage point offered him an uninterrupted view of the bar and a glittering Sydney Harbour Bridge casting sparkles on the water.

Pretty, but he wasn't here for the view. He needed to talk to fellow travellers, swapping tales of their wanderings, desperate to be distracted from the crazy thoughts that seeing Charlotte's dream house had conjured up.

A young barman sporting enough facial piercings to make him wince stopped in front of him. 'What can I get you?'

'A glass of your best Shiraz, please.'

The barman's eyebrow rose, elevating three rings higher than the rest. 'It's four hundred a glass?'

'That's fine.'

A good red would soothe his soul and loosen his tongue. Because now that he was here he didn't feel like talking all that much.

A fellow businessman in a designer suit sat on his right while an older woman in a severe black dress sat on his left. They both stared at their cells, their thumbs flying as they tapped out messages. The guy had an untouched Scotch in front of him, the woman a G&T. He recognised their harried expressions well. He usually wore one himself, striving to get deadlines done before moving on to the next challenge.

The barman didn't take long to deposit his wine in front of him and after the first sip Alex relaxed. The rich flavour of aged grapes slid over his tongue, the perfect end to a startling day.

Why had Charlotte shown him her dream house?

It was the one question that continued to bug him and raised a whole heap of other questions he'd rather not contemplate.

Did she have a hidden agenda?

Was she mistaking sex for something more?

Or was she trying to prove that, no matter how sizzling their encounters, ultimately he wouldn't be good enough to be the man she settled down with?

The latter shouldn't bother him, but it did. He'd known that feeling of worthlessness before, with his parents, where nothing he did or said seemed enough to vanquish the pall of sadness that hung over their household.

And he'd tried, boy, had he tried.

He'd got the best marks, trained hard to be chosen captain of the football team in winter, the cricket team in summer. He'd started working at the local ice-cream parlour at age fourteen to take financial pressure off them. Hell, he'd even helped shear sheep to help his dad during a busy season, when he hated those smelly woolly things.

He'd busted his ass in an effort to make his parents happy. Nothing had worked, and in the end his dad had killed himself anyway.

'Man, what a day.' The businessman on his right flung down his cell and picked up his Scotch. 'Ever feel like you're a hamster running on one of those god-damn wheels?'

Alex nodded and raised his glass. 'All the time.'

The businessman clinked his glass. 'To hamsters.'

Alex grinned and took another sip as the businessman tossed back his entire glass. He stuck out his hand. 'Alex.'

'Richard.' They shook hands before his new bestie gestured at the barman for a refill. 'You travel much?'

Alex nodded. 'All the time. I'm an accountant by trade but these days I take ailing companies and get them back on track.'

'Impressive.' Richard raised a fresh Scotch in his

direction. 'This is my fifth hotel on the eastern seaboard in ten days and, as much as I like a change, I'm exhausted.'

'What do you do?'

'CEO of my own security company. We protect anyone and anything.'

'Is that your motto?'

'It should be.' Richard took a healthy slug of his Scotch. 'Let me ask you something, Alex. Do you ever take a vacation?'

'Rarely,' Alex said, surprised the admission saddened him when he usually couldn't care less. He spent enough time on the road not to care but it struck him that sitting in hotel bars swapping stories with strangers wasn't the same as lazing by a pool reading for pleasure not business.

'You should.' Richard frowned and pinched the bridge of his nose. 'Or you'll end up like me. Wealthy but wiped out. Single and hating it.'

Alex reckoned Richard couldn't be more than fifty-five. Would that be him in another twenty-odd years, cynical but burned out, rueing his bachelorhood?

So much for bonding with fellow travellers. Richard was a real downer.

Richard wiggled his ringless third finger. 'I take it you don't have a ball and chain waiting for you at home?'

Alex shook his head. 'Footloose and fancy-free.'

Usually, he revelled in his singledom. So why did his proud declaration sound so hollow?

'I was you once, a good-looking young buck taking on the world.' Richard shrugged and downed his second Scotch in as many minutes. 'Never would've thought it'd ever lose its appeal.'

Shit. Dear old Dick was a real killjoy. 'I like being a nomad, travelling when the whim takes me, making a cool million or two.'

He threw it out there defiantly, daring Richard to disagree.

Alex liked his life. He liked living on his terms, not someone else's. As for the future, it would be solid because he'd have financial security to see him well into old age, without having to dwell on the unhappiness of his partner dragging him down.

Richard rolled his eyes and half leaned across him. 'What about you, honey? Are you a nomad too?'

Alex tried not to cringe at Richard's casual use of 'honey' for the austere businesswoman now looking down her snooty nose at the two of them.

But to his surprise, she didn't fling her drink in Richard's face as Alex half expected. Instead, she smiled and it softened the severity of the lines bracketing her mouth and eyes. 'I travel a fair bit for work but I have a doting husband waiting for me with my slippers and cigar when I get home.'

Alex laughed and Richard managed a rueful chuckle.

'Don't mind him.' Alex jerked a thumb in Richard's direction. 'I think he's had a long day.'

Richard grimaced. 'Make that a long two weeks. Hotels suck.'

The woman raised an eyebrow. 'You don't like travelling?'

'It lost its appeal a long time ago,' Richard said, studying her with open curiosity. 'What about you?'

'I love it.' Her eyes brightened with enthusiasm. 'There's nothing like a pristine hotel room at the end of a long work day or a hotel bar like this one for meeting interesting people.'

Richard grunted his disapproval and Alex nodded. 'I agree.'

'To fellow wanderers.' She tapped her wine glass against his and they both took a sip as Alex wondered if he'd stumbled into some kind of alternative reality, where the woman was the angel perched on his left shoulder and Richard the devil on his right.

The woman had a similar mind-set to him, Richard the opposite. And rather than mixing with these people bringing him the clarity he sought, he couldn't help but feel even more confused.

He could have been holed up in Charlotte's flat right now, with an armful of warm, willing woman.

Instead, he'd blown her off to reassert his independence.

What kind of an idiot did that make him?

CHAPTER TWENTY-ONE

CHARLOTTE DIDN'T WANT to be alone tonight.

With her emotions pinging all over the place after the odd evening with Alex she knew she'd be up all night, brooding and mulling.

She needed a friend. But when she'd reached out to Abby she hadn't anticipated having to meet her at the nightclub owned by Abby's boyfriend Tanner.

As she entered Embue, the *doof-doof* beat pierced her eardrums and she wished she'd stayed home after all.

This so wasn't her scene.

Beautiful people mingling, beautiful bodies dancing, making her feel decidedly ugly in her plain black dress, the only fancy outfit she owned. Like she needed a re-inforcement of how average she looked on a good day.

She'd begged off going out with Mak and Abby so many times until they'd finally left her alone. They gently teased her for being a nerd, for ending up a spinster unless she got out there and met guys. She'd laughed along with them but little did they know the real reason she remained a social hermit.

She felt lacking in all areas of her life.

Sure, she could hold her own at work, but socially she didn't know how to act or make small talk or flirt.

She'd never learned how.

Being an introvert at school ensured she'd never had friends. She'd spent the bulk of her downtime around her aunt's motley crowd: artists, musicians, flamboyant transvestites. She'd loved mingling with these interesting people but they too had made her feel insignificant. Not deliberately, but because she couldn't help but compare herself to their ostentatious lifestyles while she toiled away at her homework ensuring she achieved the dream: becoming an accountant. Woo-hoo.

But it had been more than that. She'd seen these people drift in and out of her aunt's life and figured that if her vivacious, charming aunt couldn't hold onto friends, what hope did she have?

In her experience—with her parents, with her aunt's friends, even Mak—people ultimately walked away. So it became easier to shut herself off, expecting little, giving the same.

Somewhere along the line, her self-worth had become wrapped up in this lack of serious bonding and it had spiralled out of control ever since.

She hated being a loner and feeling this unworthy but until Alex she'd felt powerless to do anything about it.

As she watched lithe, sinuous bodies wind around each other on the dance floor, a yearning so strong it took her breath away made her light-headed.

Those couples exuded sex. They wore their sexuality like a badge of honour, while she'd just given her first blowjob in the back seat of a car and skedaddled, overjoyed when Alex hadn't pushed to spend the night.

Tears stung her eyes and she blinked rapidly. Coming here had been a mistake. But falling for her fling was a much bigger one.

That was what had her so melancholy.

Pining for Alex.

Ridiculous, as she barely knew the guy and he'd made it more than clear he wasn't interested in anything more than a fling. Heck, the way he'd reacted when she'd shown him her dream house should have served as a stark warning that he could never be the guy for her.

He'd bolted because of it, had cited work as an excuse not to come home with her. Ouch. But even his obvious reticence in getting too close hadn't served to give her the wake-up call she needed.

She wanted him.

For more than a few weeks.

For the simple fact he made her feel like a different woman. A woman who could take charge in and out of the bedroom, a woman willing to step outside her comfort zone, a woman not afraid to take risks.

But it would be beyond foolish to pin her hopes of evolving into a new woman on a guy destined to leave without a backward glance. Which explained her current funk.

'Screw this,' she muttered, spinning on her low heels to head out, when she glimpsed Abby waving at her from an alcove tucked behind the main bar.

She glanced at the exit longingly, but she'd reached out to her friend and it would be poor form to ditch her now.

Squaring her shoulders, she marched through the crowd of beautiful people as if she belonged. She wished.

'I'm so glad you're here,' Abby squealed and enveloped her in a hug. 'I can't believe it's taken you this long.'

Charlotte remained silent as they disengaged and Abby waved her over to a plush gold velvet chaise longue. 'What would you like to drink?'

She bit back her first response of 'soda' and decided to live a little. 'A vodka and lime, please.'

'Coming right up.' Abby spoke into a Bluetooth-thingy clipped onto her collar.

'What is that?'

Rueful, Abby shrugged. 'Tanner sets me up in here so I don't have to fight my way to the bar.'

'And fend off the inevitable guys who'd flock to you,' she said drily, garnering a laugh from her friend.

'You might think he's possessive, I prefer to think of him as protective.'

'He's a good guy,' Charlotte said, though she wouldn't admit in a million years that she found Tanner intimidating.

With all those tattoos and that perpetual glower she found him formidable. Sexy, but scary. She could never handle a guy like that but her friend did it with ease.

'Yeah, he is.' Abby's eyes gleamed whenever she mentioned her boyfriend. She got that glow, the kind that could never be emulated by any skincare. 'So what's happening with you and that dishy boss?'

'We're hanging out,' Charlotte said, and promptly burst into tears.

'Oh, no, honey.' Abby pulled her into her arms, squeezing tight, while Charlotte cried out some of the tension making her feel so confused.

She rarely cried. She'd learned from a young age that tears were futile and did nothing but make her look puffy-eyed. She'd cried a lot when her parents had first left her with Dee but her aunt had never mentioned her red, swollen eyes.

Instead, Dee would ply her with sodas and cupcakes, and cuddle her incessantly to make up for her parents' callous disregard of a child's tender feelings. In the ensuing years, when her parents hadn't come back no matter how hard she'd sobbed into her pillow at night, her tears had eventually dried.

So finding herself in the midst of a crying jag was as disorientating as discovering she might be falling for her fling.

Abby didn't say anything, just held her, until her sobs petered out.

'Sorry about that,' Charlotte said, when her friend released her. She scavenged for tissues in her handbag and tidied up her face as best she could, knowing she must look a fright but was too drained to care. 'Must be that time of the month.'

Abby's raised eyebrows implied she didn't buy her pathetic excuse for a second. Their drinks appearing saved Charlotte from having to say anything for a moment but the second the waiter disappeared Abby swooped.

'Okay, start talking and don't stop 'til you've told me everything.'

'Not much to tell.' Ha. Understatement of the year.

'Last time we spoke, you'd had sex with him at that warehouse before you knew he was your boss.' Abby pinned her with a probing stare. 'I'm assuming you've done the dirty again?'

Charlotte sighed, hating the inevitable twang in her

chest whenever she thought about the connection she shared with Alex. 'Several times.'

'And?'

'And I said I was okay with a fling but I don't think I'm built that way.' She ended on an embarrassing hiccup and squeezed her eyes shut to stave off more tears.

'Oh, Char.' Abby draped an arm over her shoulders and squeezed before releasing her.

When Charlotte opened her eyes, Abby stared at her with determination.

'Hope you don't mind, but I'm your friend and I'm going to be blunt, okay?'

Even the mention of blunt had her remembering Alex saying that was one of the traits he liked about her. She wondered how much he'd like it when she channelled that signature bluntness into dumping his ass before she got in any deeper.

'Do your worst.'

'For as long as I've known you, you've never been out with a guy. You don't date. You don't socialise. Don't you think letting go a little with this guy, who obviously pushed your buttons enough you had sex with him on first meeting, is a good thing?' Abby hesitated, plucking at her bottom lip, before continuing. 'I know you envisage the grand happily-ever-after. We all do. It's in our DNA or something. But having a fling before you settle down can be the best thing for you.'

'You're right, I know you're right.'

Hadn't Charlotte given herself the very same pep talk? But using cool logic to explain away her raunchy behaviour and keeping Alex at an emotional distance seemed much easier in theory.

'Maybe I'm confusing lust with a stronger emotion?'

Charlotte shrugged, as if her concerns meant little when in fact she needed all the help she could get. 'I've never felt this way about a guy before so perhaps I'm in over my head?'

And terrified that, no matter how hard she tried to dress up this thing with Alex as a fling, she'd find it difficult to walk away at the end.

A frown slashed Abby's brow. 'Have you discussed your fears with him?'

'Hell no. He'd end things instantly.' She screwed up her nose. 'Alex is a "no muss no fuss" kind of guy. He travels a lot. Doesn't stay in one place too long.'

Abby nodded, ponderous. 'And he's been upfront with you from the start about an expiration date on this fling?'

'Uh-huh.'

'Hmm...' Abby sipped at her cocktail, some bright pink thing with bubbles that would give Charlotte an instant headache. 'Honestly, Char, I don't know what to say. I want you to keep having fun with this guy because it's good for you. But your tears indicate you're already emotionally invested, which can only end badly for you when he leaves.'

Charlotte managed a watery smile. 'You've just articulated exactly how I feel. But without giving me a solution.'

Abby took another healthy slurp of her cocktail, like the alcohol would give her clarity. 'Is there any chance... I mean, do you think he feels more for you beyond the obvious?'

In her more deluded moments, when he cradled her in his arms as if he never wanted to let go, Charlotte liked to think so.

But she'd given up believing in fairy tales a long time ago, around the time her folks dumped her with her weird aunt so they could travel the world, and the only fantasies she believed in these days occurred between the pages of her favourite novels.

'He's made it more than clear we're short-term, nothing more,' she said, wincing. The facts hurt.

'Then you've got a decision to make,' Abby said, clasping her hand and squeezing. 'Keep having fun and take what you can get. Or end it now before you get hurt.'

Charlotte smiled in gratitude at her friend, not stating the obvious.

What if it was already too late?

CHAPTER TWENTY-TWO

HANGING OUT IN the hotel bar last Friday night hadn't given Alex the emotional distance he'd needed from Charlotte. In fact, it had only served to reinforce how much that part of his life had lost its appeal. Not good.

So he reserved his cowardice for the office and ensured he avoided her all week.

Sure, they discussed work projects when needed but he told her he needed time to organise the new staffing hierarchy going forward and thankfully she believed him.

He'd referred three new clients to her too, all involving a lot of work to ensure she stayed busy.

And stayed away from him.

But all that was about to change because somehow he'd been so swamped for the last few hours that he hadn't noticed the time and now they were the last two people in the office on a Friday night again.

Damn.

He remembered the last time this had happened, every erotic moment replaying in his mind like a dirty movie.

His cock thickened just thinking about it and he snuck a surreptitious glance at her as she crossed the outer office to the photocopier.

There was nothing remotely remarkable about her outfit today. Calf-length navy skirt. Pale blue shirt. Negligible heels on navy pumps. She fitted the stereotype of a dedicated accountant but he knew what lay beneath that sedate exterior and he clenched his hands into fists to stop from barging out there and tearing off her outer layers.

She stabbed at a few buttons on the photocopier then leaned forward, drawing the skirt tight across her ass. Alex bit back a groan, his cock at full attention now and making sitting uncomfortable.

He couldn't see a panty line at this distance and imagined her wearing a thong. Black satin. Smooth. Slippery. Easy to hook aside as he spread her legs wide, bent her over that copier and entered her...

Fuck.

He stood and stalked around his desk, chastising himself for being a fool but unable to stop this relentless desire for her.

She chose that moment to glance over her shoulder, her gaze knowing, as if she knew he'd been watching her.

He made it as far as the door to his office when her bold stare zeroed in on his cock, an obvious bulge in his trousers.

Her tongue darted out to sweep her bottom lip in a gesture so provocative he felt it all the way to his balls.

This woman was fire and ice.

Hot and cold.

Temptation and reservation.

She was something else.

His cell rang at that moment. A smart guy would have ignored it and followed through on the lust pound-

ing through every inch of him. But he'd turned into a
dumb schmuck lately and the cause was staring at him
with a beguiling mix of daring and defiance.

Taunting him. Challenging him.

So much for avoiding her. He wanted her so damn
badly his vision clouded with it.

But giving in now wouldn't end well for either of
them, not when he knew in his gut that Charlie wanted
more from him than he could give, so he managed a
terse nod, swung around and closed the office door.

'This is bullshit,' Charlotte muttered, furious for allow-
ing herself to be dragged into Alex's stupid game again.

He'd been doing this all freaking week, business one
minute, casting lustful glances her way the next.

She. Was. Over. It.

They couldn't go on this way. Something would snap.
She had a sneaking suspicion it would be her. Or his
neck if he ever let her close enough again to wrap her
hands around it.

Not that she didn't appreciate his faith in her work
ethic. She'd never been so challenged professionally,
with the three clients he'd referred her way taking up
most of her time. With a little luck she'd be in line for
a big promotion to the coveted managerial role that
would ensure she could afford her upcoming mortgage
and then some.

She had a feeling he was grooming her for it and
while she understood his reticence for discussing it, she
couldn't help but hope. But all the work in the world
couldn't distract from how much she missed their physical contact, how much she craved his touch.

It wouldn't be so bad if she didn't have to see him

every day, strutting around the office in those designer suits that moulded his body to perfection, smiling at everyone, being charming and affable because that was who he was.

What would it be like to be that confident? To draw people to you without trying? To be a natural extrovert who never knew the agony of uncertainty and awkwardness?

She'd accepted who she was a long time ago but she'd be lying if she didn't admit to being a tad jealous of people like Alex who breezed through life without a care in the world.

So after a long week she'd decided to stay behind tonight in the hope they could have a word. Maybe get supper together. Maybe indulge in something more.

Because she'd come to a decision after her chat with Abby last Friday.

She would take what she could get while she could and ensure she waved Alex away with a light heart when he walked out of her life.

She'd wanted this.

She'd called the shots at the start.

No use getting the proverbial cold feet because her long-term dreams and her current fantasies had got mixed up.

Clarity wouldn't come from mulling and second-guessing.

Clarity would come from screwing her brains out and walking away from this fling a well-satisfied woman.

She'd sensed him watching her earlier, had been delighted to discover he still wanted her as badly as she wanted him, the evidence of his desire making her salivate.

But he'd closed the door on her, deliberately shutting her out.

'Good luck with that, buddy,' she said, kicking at a leg on her desk as she channelled her indignation into tidying up.

She wanted to be ready to execute her plan the moment he tried to make his escape.

He made her wait a full twenty minutes before exiting his office. He paused on the threshold, uncertain, as he glanced at her picking up her satchel and turning off her office light. She kept her back to him, not wanting him to see the first part of her plan until it was time.

He didn't move as she headed for the elevator.

If he didn't follow her in, her plan would be scuttled. But it would also be a good indication that maybe she'd read this situation all wrong and he'd cooled things off between them ahead of schedule.

She pressed the elevator button to go down and by the time it arrived and the doors slid open, he still hadn't moved.

She stepped inside, thankful this old building didn't have cameras in the elevators, and held the button to keep the doors open.

Then she turned around.

His eyes bugged as he caught sight of her blouse, unbuttoned to the waist, revealing a sheer creamy lace bra.

She'd been wearing provocative lingerie all week in the hope he might get to see it and if this didn't do the trick, nothing would.

Her finger cramped from pressing the elevator button and just when she'd given up hope he bounded towards her and almost skidded into the elevator in his haste to join her.

'Going down?' She arched an eyebrow, biting back a triumphant smile as he launched at her. One hand splayed behind her head, the other on her ass, his lips crushing hers.

Her finger slipped off the button as he backed them into the corner of the elevator, his hard cock hitting her sweet spot and making her whimper.

He ravaged her mouth as she clung to him, devouring her as if he'd never get enough. Nipping at her bottom lip. His tongue sweeping into her mouth. Challenging. Commanding.

Charlotte was so damned turned on she momentarily wondered if she could come from kissing alone. But then he wrenched his mouth from hers, pausing long enough to hit the stop button. The elevator juddered to a halt but they were just getting started.

'You are so fucking hot,' he murmured, rucking up her skirt and smoothing his palms up her thighs. 'Do you have any idea what you do to me?'

She palmed his cock through his trousers. 'I think I do.'

He plucked at her panties, almost tearing them off in his haste, his urgency delighting her. Emboldened by his obvious desire, she unzipped him and slipped her hand in. 'I want you inside me. Now.'

He slipped a finger between her slick folds, another, and groaned. 'You're certainly ready for me.'

She bit back her retort, 'always', because that sounded too permanent and she didn't want to scare him off, not when she wanted him this badly.

'So wet, so sweet.' His fingers slid in and out, sweeping over her clit every third stroke, before gliding in again. Sure, masterful strokes designed to ratchet her excitement to unbearable levels.

'Inside. Now,' she gasped, as he slipped a third finger inside her, stretching her, alighting her nerve endings.

He claimed her mouth again as he sheathed himself in record time before plunging into her to the hilt. The back of her head thunked against the elevator wall. She didn't care, the fleeting pain diluted in a wave of pleasure spreading from her core upward.

He plundered her mouth as his fingers clamped onto her ass, hoisting her higher so she could wrap her legs around him. He thrust into her repeatedly, thick and long and oh, so good. Filling her in a way she'd never imagined in her wildest dreams.

With every slide out, with every thrust in, he hit her sweet spot. Over and over until she hovered on the edge of an orgasm so powerful her back spasmed.

Then he changed the angle of his hips and she plummeted over and into a free fall of carnal bliss so intense she screamed.

He kissed her, swallowing her cries of release and groaning his own into her mouth, his fingers digging into her ass so tight she'd have bruises for sure.

She didn't care. She didn't care about anything right now but the way Alex made her feel, wishing she could feel this good all the time.

'How long are you staying around for now?'

The moment the question slipped from her lips she regretted it. In her post-sex stupor she'd overstepped a line they'd agreed on at the start. And in adding in that one significant word 'now' she'd implied that because of their involvement he'd extend his time in Sydney.

Crap, she'd screwed up, big time.

'I'll be gone once the project here is done, another few weeks max,' he said, his cool tone chilling her as he withdrew from her, physically and emotionally.

He turned away, giving her time to fix herself up. How kind of him. A gentleman now that he'd had his way with her.

Okay, so that was grossly unfair. She'd seduced him and when he shut down as she'd expected she blamed him.

'Can you press the button, please? I need to get home.' She sounded so prim, so proper, she inwardly cringed.

'Sure.'

The elevator lurched as it started its descent again as they stood side by side, watching those infernal numbers count down.

How could they have such a strong physical connection but anything further resulted in this frigid stand-off?

When the doors opened into the car park and they stepped out, Charlotte mustered her best nonchalant expression. 'See you tomorrow—'

He kissed her, a mere brush of his lips against hers, his tenderness almost undoing her completely.

When he pulled back, she couldn't read the turmoil of emotion darkening his eyes. 'I'm taking you out on a date tomorrow night. Pick you up at your place around seven.'

With that, he spun on his heel, leaving her confused and gaping and wondering what the hell had just happened.

CHAPTER TWENTY-THREE

ALEX HAD NEVER been so torn in all his life.

He wanted to give Charlotte a night she'd never forget.

He wanted to let her down gently.

He wanted to express how incredible she made him feel but that it had to end.

He knew that, after last night. The moment she'd asked how long he'd be staying around for, he'd known. She'd invested far too much into this fling and the damnedest thing was, maybe he had too.

Easier to break it off now, before he ended up breaking her heart.

He didn't want to hurt her. She was too special for that. And he knew that was exactly what would happen if they continued spending time together.

The sex was sensational but somehow, whenever they hooked up, he was left wanting more and if her post-coital question in that elevator was any indication, she did too.

She'd left him no choice.

He had to end it.

Tonight.

He could have done it last night but it would have been too callous after they'd just had sex. Besides, he

knew Charlotte was a hearts and flowers kind of girl.
That damn house she coveted so badly told him that.

So that was what he'd give her tonight. A night of romance, a night a special woman like her deserved. Then
he'd take her home, give her a chaste kiss, and end it.

She'd understand. They'd both known the fleeting
nature of this going in and he hoped that once she got
the promotion she'd be too busy to give him the evil
eye at work.

Another two weeks and he'd be out of here, leaving
Sydney behind and heading to Auckland for a conference before weighing up his options. He had companies in Perth, Adelaide and Melbourne begging for his
attention and he hadn't decided which one to tackle
first. Maybe Perth would be the best option, the other
side of the country so he wouldn't be tempted to hop
on a plane and return to Sydney if he lost his mind and
ended up pining for Charlie.

'Idiot,' he muttered, jabbing at her doorbell.

He had a clear-cut plan.

He had to stick to it.

The door opened and he sucked in a breath. Charlotte
stood before him wearing a purple strapless mini dress
that hugged every curve of her body. She'd curled her
hair and it fell in soft waves over her shoulders. She'd
used smoky make-up on her eyes and a plum gloss that
made her lips shimmer.

Fuck. She was a knockout, determined to shatter his
limited self-control.

He couldn't screw her tonight, it wouldn't be right,
but damn it was going to be hard to keep his hands off
her when every cell in his body clamoured to be all
over her.

'You look incredible,' he finally said, when he un-glued his tongue from the roof of his mouth and stepped forward to place a kiss on her cheek. 'Stunning.'

'Thanks.' She blushed and tugged on the hem of the dress self-consciously. 'My flatmate left a stack of dresses behind when she moved to New York so I raided her wardrobe.'

He bit back his first response, 'You should do it more often,' for the simple fact he wouldn't be the benefi-ciary of seeing her metamorphose into a sex goddess after tonight.

The thought left him feeling winded.

Thankfully, she didn't notice anything amiss as she turned to grab a black clutch and her keys off the hall table. When she turned back he'd managed to get him-self under control and forced a lazy grin that belied the churning in his gut.

'Where are we going?'

'It's a surprise,' he said, placing a hand in the small of her back and guiding her down the path towards his car. He could feel the heat of her skin through the thin material. It didn't help his rampant libido straining to let loose.

'I'm not usually one for surprises but in your case I'll make an exception.' She cast him a flirtatious glance from beneath mascaraed lashes and damned if he didn't want to drag her into the back seat again.

'Are you flirting with me, Miss Baxter?'

'I may be, Mr Bronson.'

He opened the passenger door and waited for her to slide in before leaning down. 'You're something else. You know that, right?'

An odd melancholy clouded her eyes, as if she sensed

this would be their last hurrah. 'I'm hoping you mean that in the nicest way possible.'

'I do,' he said, startled to inadvertently recite those two little words that personally terrified him.

He slammed the door and stalked around the car, determined to keep this evening light-hearted. It was the least he could do before letting down the first woman he'd actually cared about in a long time, if ever.

They made desultory small talk on the short drive to the exclusive harbourside restaurant where he'd made reservations. When they pulled up out front and he handed over his keys to have his car valet parked, her eyebrows rose.

'I heard it takes a year to get into this place. How did you manage it?'

He tapped the side of his nose and winked. 'It's not what you know, it's who you know.'

When she continued to eye him with suspicion, he said, 'I called in a favour from an old buddy.' He quickly added, 'And before you think I bring all my dates here, you're the first.'

'I'm flattered,' she said, but didn't sound like it. In fact, ever since they'd arrived here, she'd seemed uneasy.

He waited until she'd stepped from the car before asking, 'What's wrong?'

She hesitated, as if unsure how to answer. 'Don't get me wrong, I think it's fantastic you brought me here, but I guess it just reinforces that once I buy the house I'll never have a chance to do fancy stuff like this.'

Of all the things she could have said, he hadn't expected that. He didn't want to have any deep and meaningful conversations tonight. He wanted her to have fun so she'd remember him fondly and not as the asshole who dumped her.

Her response virtually echoed the concerns he'd expressed when she'd shown him her future home.

Had she actually heard what he'd said and was reconsidering making such a huge commitment before she'd experienced all that life had to offer?

A flare of hope had him wondering what it would be like to be around for her awakening, before he mentally kicked himself in the ass for going there.

Even if Charlotte had reconsidered taking on a huge mortgage, that didn't mean he'd be up for anything beyond short-term. Whatever the time limit on their relationship, he'd eventually end up leaving; and eventually breaking her heart. No way in hell would he be responsible for that.

Determined to make tonight special for her, he smiled. 'You'll be whipping up fancy meals in your very own kitchen. How cool will that be?'

She managed a wobbly smile. 'You're right. Maybe I'm being a chicken because I'm going to put down a deposit next week.'

'That soon?'

Why did the thought leave him so hollow?

She nodded. 'It's exciting yet terrifying at the same time.'

Her bottom lip wobbled a tad and he captured her chin in his hand, tilting it up slightly. 'Hey. This is your dream. Don't ever doubt yourself, because you're incredible and you can do anything you damn well set your mind to.'

A fact he was all too aware of as she stared at him in open adoration.

Fuck. He'd been so intent on not breaking her heart some time down the track, what if it was too late?

'Let's eat,' he said, sounding gruff as he released her, but as they entered the restaurant he couldn't shake the feeling that no matter how special he tried to make tonight, it wouldn't make an ounce of difference.

She'd end up hating him by the end of it regardless.

They reverted to small talk after they ordered: the rosemary-skewered Tasmanian salmon with a cauliflower cumin salad for him, the oven-roasted pork belly with a semi-dried tomato mousse for her. The meals arrived surprisingly fast and he watched Charlotte devour hers. He loved her healthy appetite: in all areas of her life.

Sadly, he couldn't taste a thing. Because the longer he sat across from her pretending this was just a regular date between two people who were crazy about each other, the harder it was to fathom that they wouldn't be indulging in this banter any longer. That he wouldn't be able to kiss her, to touch her, to bury himself deep inside her.

This was bullshit.

Of his own making.

'What's wrong?' She placed her fork and knife neatly together in the centre of her empty plate and nudged it away. 'You're distracted.'

'Sorry.' He grimaced, not wanting to tell her the truth now, like this, but finding it increasingly difficult to hold back.

'Is it work? Is there a problem?' She gestured around the restaurant, featuring floor-to-ceiling windows with stunning views of Sydney by night, the glow from nearby buildings reflecting off the water like glittering fairy lights. 'Is that why you brought me here, to soften me up before you deliver bad news?'

He shook his head. 'Nothing like that.'

'Then what?'

She searched his face for answers he was reluctant to give. Hell, they hadn't even made it to dessert yet.

'I wanted tonight to be special.' And that was all she'd be getting out of him until he took her home. This wasn't the place to break unpleasant news.

Her eyes narrowed slightly. 'There's more.'

He should have known she'd be intuitive, picking up on his mood no matter how hard he tried to hide it.

Thankfully, her cell rang at that moment, a momentary reprieve as he gathered his thoughts.

She quickly glanced at it, one eyebrow rising. 'Sorry, I have to take this, it's my aunt.'

'Go ahead,' he said, pushing away his half-eaten meal.

He watched her expression change from happiness at hearing from her aunt to concern, though he couldn't hear much of her murmured conversation as a pianist started up.

When she hung up, her cute nose crinkled. 'I'm sorry to do this after you went to all the trouble of getting us a booking here, but I have to go home.'

'Is everything all right?'

'My aunt's biggest client, a regular who keeps her in business, has an urgent order to be filled and I have to do it tonight to ship first thing in the morning.'

He tried not to laugh.

Her aunt's kinky sex-toy business had saved him from blurting the truth here. But his relief was short-lived, that phone call only delaying the inevitable.

'Do you mind if we leave now? As it is it's going to take me all night to sort everything.'

'Sure,' he said, gesturing at a waiter for the bill. He wanted to offer to help but he knew that spending the next few hours beside her as she sorted through that quirky lingerie and more wouldn't be conducive to ending things. 'Let's go.'

She worked on her cell for the entire drive back to her flat, doing an online search for the courier companies her aunt usually used, making bookings.

It gave him a chance to mentally rehearse what he'd say when they arrived at her flat but he never got the chance because her cell rang again when they reached her doorstep, her aunt issuing more orders.

When she hung up, she pecked him on the lips. 'Sorry, I really have to get started. I'll see you tomorrow.'

With that, she left him staring at a closed door.

So much for manning up and ending it tonight. He'd have to psych himself up another time.

Sooner rather than later.

CHAPTER TWENTY-FOUR

As if Charlotte needed a reminder of how thought-ful Alex was, he sent her a text the next morning say-ing she could take the day off if she needed it after her all-nighter.

Considering she'd got a grand total of two hours' sleep once she'd filled the massive order for her aunt's business, she took it. She fired back a quick Thx, am ex-hausted, will c u soon. Meaning tomorrow. Or tonight, if she plucked up the courage to text him later this af-ternoon and ask him to come over.

She didn't like how they'd ended things last night.

He'd obviously gone to a lot of trouble to organise a special dinner date for her but she'd sensed his reticence at the restaurant, as if something was bothering him.

She'd caught him staring at her a few times when he'd thought she wasn't looking and she hadn't been able to fathom the odd look in his eyes.

He'd been about to open up to her, she just knew it, when her aunt had called, and while she loved Dee she could have strangled her at that moment. He hadn't of-fered to help her either, which was another red flag.

What was going on inside that handsome head of his?

Increasingly sleepy, Charlotte curled up in bed, read

three-quarters of the latest bonkbuster that had her
riveted and dozed for an hour or so. When she woke,
morning had given way to afternoon and she felt as
lacklustre as she had before sleep.

Something kept niggling at her, something about last
night, a feeling she hadn't been able to shake since she
entered that fancy restaurant.

It bordered on…disappointment. That she'd never be
able to do anything like that again. That she was giving
up a lot for her dream house—like expensive dinners
and spa days and vacations—and ultimately, she wondered whether the sacrifices would be worth it.

She wanted that house. Craved it. Damn Alex for
planting those thoughts in her head, that she'd be missing out on something if a house financially tethered
her for life.

Only one way to shake off her funk.

Visit her baby.

So for the umpteenth time over the last few weeks
she found herself parked opposite the Californian bungalow that had captivated her from the first moment
she saw it online.

She could see her life behind that picket fence so
clearly.

Coming home at the end of a long day, letting herself in the front door, toeing off her shoes and padding
barefoot along the polished, honey-coloured boards to
the cosy kitchen where she'd pour a glass of wine before sinking into her sofa in the lounge room.

The lounge had an open fireplace and, while Sydney
winters weren't terribly cold, she couldn't wait to curl
up with a book in front of it.

Throw in the stand-alone clawfoot bath that was big

enough for two people and a modern double shower, a small sunroom that backed onto a tiny cottage garden and a reading nook on the veranda she'd immediately coveted, and she could hardly wait.

As she continued to stare at her dream house, she waited for the inevitable buzz of excitement, that slightly breathless feeling that made her tingle every time she visited.

Today, it didn't come.

Probably overtired, she knuckled her eyes, yawned, took a deep breath and stretched.

It didn't help.

Odd. Her house—she'd come to think of it as hers the last few days as she finalised her mortgage at the bank—appeared as charming as ever. She loved the ecru-trimmed windows, the fresh painted exterior, the duck-egg-blue fence. It looked like a home, not just a house, the kind of home she'd craved since she was a child, her nose buried in a book while Dee chattered incessantly, choosing to live in fictional worlds rather than her own where her parents didn't give a damn about her and preferred living in a tent than in a proper house with their own daughter.

But as she stared at her house, the doubts crept in.

Was she doing the right thing? Tying herself to a life of debt with no money left over for travel or indulgences? Ensuring that bricks and mortar consumed her life? Making sure she did it tough until she found the dream man to fulfil the rest of her fantasy and help shoulder the load?

What if that didn't happen? Or what if the guy she met didn't want to live in this house? What if he didn't want to take on the responsibility of a big mortgage alongside her? What if he preferred going out to frugal dinners at home?

A wave of nausea swept over her and she swallowed.

She'd had it clearly planned out. Get the house first; the rest would follow. A carefully calculated decision she'd been more than happy about.

Until Alex.

He'd done this to her. He had her wishing for things she'd never wanted before. Fun. Frivolity. Fantasies…

'Damn you,' she muttered under her breath, thumping the steering wheel for good measure.

It didn't help. Sadly, she had a feeling nothing would because, no matter how many times she envisaged her life in this house, she couldn't help but see Alex, in the garden, in the kitchen, in the bedroom, front and centre in her happily-ever-after scenario.

And he'd made it more than clear that would never, ever happen.

Which left her totally screwed.

CHAPTER TWENTY-FIVE

ALEX KNEW HE was in big trouble when he mooned around the office for the entire day, unable to concentrate on work because Charlotte wasn't around.

Pathetic.

Since when had he turned into some lovesick schmuck who couldn't think about anything but a woman?

*Love*sick?

Fuck. The moment the word popped into his head, he knew he had to get out of here. Had to do something drastic to shake himself up.

He didn't love Charlotte.

He didn't have it in him to love anyone.

Not any more.

So he did the one thing guaranteed to give him the wake-up call he needed.

Booked a trip home.

It would take too long to drive to the tiny outback town not far from Broken Hill, the isolated mining town over seven hundred miles west of Sydney, so he booked a flight leaving that night and made arrangements to be away from work for two days.

It was a crazy, impulsive thing to do, considering he hadn't been back to Rocky Plains since his father's funeral many years ago and had vowed then never to return.

But he needed to do this. Needed a reminder of why he could never have what Charlie wanted.

Charlie… He should tell her he was leaving. Then again, they had a casual thing. He didn't owe her any explanations and it sure as hell wouldn't make their imminent break-up any easier if he started treating her like a girlfriend he had to check in with.

Scowling, he gathered his things, gave curt instructions to the receptionist regarding the work to be delegated, and headed for the airport. He didn't even stop at his hotel to pack. He wouldn't be staying in Rocky Plains long enough to warrant a bag.

At the airport he flipped his cell over and over in his hand, wondering if he should give his mum a heads-up of his impending arrival, before ultimately deciding against it.

She wouldn't care one way or the other if he showed up. She never had, not since he'd left home for university without looking back.

They had a polite relationship. One maintained out of obligation rather than any real emotion. He knew why.

He couldn't help but blame himself for his father's death and couldn't bear to see the judgement in his mother's all-knowing stare, like she blamed him too.

Even if the coroner and local police force had been unable to establish whether his father had drowned in the family dam by accident or had committed suicide, Alex knew the truth.

His dad had lost the will to live a long time ago.

He'd seen evidence of it every single miserable day,

growing up in a household where his dad couldn't give a flying fuck about him no matter how hard he tried and his parents hated each other yet did their utmost to hide it.

The flight took two and a half hours and landed in Broken Hill around eight p.m. As he stepped off the small plane, the heat hit him first. Descending like a heavy, oppressive cloak, stifling every living thing beneath it.

He'd travelled the world and had welcomed the warmth of the tropics. But the outback heat was something else entirely and it made him want to claw off his tie and guzzle a litre of water.

He hired a car, made the thirty-minute drive to Rocky Plains and checked in to the first motel he could find, then spent an hour lying on the rickety bed, staring at a ceiling mottled by water stains. Rain in these parts was rare but when it came it bucketed down in a relentless torrent.

He hadn't thought this through.

Back in Sydney, he'd been so desperate for a reality check that he'd bolted. Now that he was here, listening to the raucous laughter of beer drinkers from the bar next door and the occasional hoon doing burnouts up the main street, he wished he'd never come.

He must have fallen asleep from sheer exhaustion and over-thinking at some point, because when he woke sunlight streamed through the dirty window set high in the wall.

Time to head home and face his mother.

After grabbing an OJ from the motel's vending machine, he drove the ten minutes to his family's farm. Not a working farm, per se, just a small homestead, a barn and a dam on a few acres of land stuck in the middle of nowhere.

He hated it.

The isolation had always got to him and being an only child hadn't helped. When he wasn't being forced to endure his parents' less than scintillating company he'd been left to wander alone. Riding his dirt bike along tracks. Taking pot-shots at cans with an air rifle. Swimming in the dam.

His heart sank as he turned into the pocked drive. He'd never understand why his mother had chosen to stay here after his dad's death, stuck in the middle of nowhere, left to wallow in bad memories.

She'd be home. She always was. His dad had worked on the railway in Broken Hill; she'd tutored kids online. It had worked, until his dad had lost his job and ended up moping around the house.

That was when things had turned really ugly and he'd been glad to finish high school the year after and escape.

She must have heard the car because by the time he'd parked and got out she stood on the back step, waving at him.

He didn't deserve the huge smile that lit her face. He didn't deserve anything bar a scathing lecture for being such a shitty son.

His feet dragged, just as they used to, as he approached the back veranda. 'Hey, Mum.'

Her smile widened. 'This is a nice surprise.'

In the few seconds before she enveloped him in a hug, he noticed several things. Her greying hair had been coloured a natural-looking blonde that softened her face. She wore make-up. And the perpetual frown lines that resided between her brows had eased.

His mum looked younger than the last time he'd seen her two years ago. The last time he'd flown her to Brisbane for three days, part of his obligatory son duties. She'd sensed his heart wasn't in it, like the other times he'd made the hollow gesture and she'd returned home after one night. He didn't blame her. He'd felt nothing but relief.

She'd mentioned a new man in her life back then, a new pub owner in town. He hadn't wanted to know the details but had wished her well. If anyone deserved happiness after the shit she'd put up with over the years because of his dad, she did.

When she wrapped her arms around him and the faintest waft of cinnamon reached his nose, he had a sudden urge to bawl. He clung to her, his intention to keep their reunion brief lost amid a wave of emotion he could almost label regret.

Why had he stayed away so long?

When she released him, her eyes were damp. 'Come in and I'll make you a cuppa.'

He had a hankering for something a lot stronger but tea would do for now. As he stepped inside, he was catapulted back in time. He remembered entering this kitchen every day after school, ravenous for his mum's delicious baking but eager to escape to avoid the inevitable awkwardness between his folks after his father lost his job. He'd cram choc-chip cookies in his mouth, snaffle a few for later, drink half a carton of milk, then bolt for his room on the pretext of homework. He'd keep his ears plugged to drown out potential arguments. Would listen to music half the night. Had done whatever it took to cope.

'Are you going to stand there all day?'

He blinked, to find himself still hovering in the doorway, and shook his head slightly to clear it. 'Memories,' he said, entering the kitchen and inhaling deeply. 'Still smells amazing in here.'

'That's because I bake every day.' She bustled around the kitchen, the familiarity of her movements making his throat clog so badly no amount of clearing would ease it. 'Not for me, of course, but I donate baked goods to the church every week and they sell them.'

Alex hated his first thought: why was she so altruistic now when she had barely been able to utter a civil word to his father all those years ago?

'So what brings you by?' She placed a cup of tea in front of him, along with a plate piled high with cookies, a slice of apple cake and a lamington. 'Is something wrong?'

Of course she'd jump to that conclusion. He never came home.

'Everything's fine, Mum.' Her baking smelled divine but he lost his appetite as he realised he'd have to give her some semblance of the truth to explain his unexpected arrival. 'But I realised I've been avoiding this place for a long time now…and I wanted to see you,' he belatedly added, feeling like a bastard when her face fell.

'Well, whatever your reasons, I'm glad you're here.' She sat opposite and sipped her tea, wariness in her gaze as she studied him. 'It's been too long.'

Her subtle chastisement hung between them and he searched for the right words to make her understand why he'd stayed away. Bitterness, resentment and a long-festering indignation burned in his gut, making him feel slightly sick.

'Why did you stay, Mum?'

He blurted the question, unable to remain silent a moment longer. He wanted to ask her so much about the past but knew it would be futile. What was the point of dredging up rotten memories that would only serve to drag them both down?

But he had to know the answer to this one question. Had to know why she'd chosen to stay when he couldn't wait to get away.

'Because this is my home,' she said, with a shrug. She stared into her tea, unable to meet his gaze, her mouth downturned. 'I loved it. I always loved it, even when your father was around and trying his best to make me hate it.'

She lifted her head to eyeball him, her stare surprisingly defiant. 'I stay here because it reminds me of how much I tolerated and how far I've come.' She tapped her chest. 'I'm proud of being a fighter, not a quitter.'

Like you.

Though she didn't say it, he saw the accusation in her eyes and it served like a kick in the guts.

'I didn't quit, Mum. I chose to walk away from a place that held nothing but bad memories.' He gestured around the kitchen. 'You chose to stay for your reasons, I chose to leave for mine, so don't make me feel bad because of it.'

She deflated a little. 'I'm not trying to make you feel bad.' She shook her head, tendrils that had escaped her ponytail clinging to her face. 'I just can't understand why you stayed away so long, why you didn't come back to see me.'

Her voice rose and ended on a squeak she quickly covered with a cough. 'I'm not laying a guilt trip on you.

I appreciated those plane tickets you bought me over the years so we could catch up in the city. But I guess I just really want to know why you've returned now.' She held up her hand before he could respond. 'And don't give me some cock and bull story about wanting to see me, because if you'd wanted to do that you would've visited any time over the last two years since I last saw you.'

Suitably chastised, and fast running out of excuses, he folded his arms and compressed his lips into a mutinous line.

She guffawed, a loud bark of laughter he'd rarely heard from his mother growing up. 'Your father used to get the same stubborn expression when I asked him a question he didn't want to answer.'

Alex didn't want to revisit the past but his mum had given him the perfect opening and he took it. 'Did Dad kill himself?'

Shadows descended over his mum's eyes, blanketing the earlier defiance. But he had to know. His original intention to come here, to remind himself why he could never lead a staid life stuck in one place too long, had been briefly superseded by his thirst for the truth. Growing up in this household, stifled by moroseness, hadn't been healthy. Getting answers could be nothing but cathartic.

'I can't say for certain but from his mind-set in the days leading up to his death, yes, I think he committed suicide.'

How could his mum sound so stoic? As if she were chatting about their pet dog that had accidentally drowned in the dam years before his dad.

'What was different about those days before he died?'

Alex couldn't let it go, no matter how much he feared the answers.

'Your father suffered from depression, as you know—'

'Actually, Mum, I didn't know, because both of you pussyfooted around the issue in front of me. You stomped around here with a stern face and Dad slunk around like he was scared of his own shadow. I frigging hated it!'

His mum blanched, staring at him with hollow eyes, devastation etched into every line on her face, as if he were a stranger. Which technically, he was. In staying away all these years for his own peace of mind, he hadn't stopped once to think how it had affected hers. She'd always sounded so calm during their chats on the phone, cool to the point of detachment when she came to the city, like she didn't care whether she had a son or not.

But maybe she'd done the same as him, withdrawn, removing herself from the situation emotionally rather than physically.

'I didn't want you to bear the brunt of it like I did,' she said, so softly her voice quavered. 'I tried to hide so much of his behaviour from you.'

A sliver of foreboding pierced his resolve to know the truth. 'What behaviour?'

She sighed, her shoulders slumping as she hugged her middle. 'Your father always had depression. I knew it when I married him and in a way that quiet staidness about him drew me in. He always medicated to stay on top of it, but after he lost his job on the railway and was home all the time he cut back. Said the meds were affecting his taste and sight and other aspects of his life.'

She blushed and Alex really didn't want to go there. 'The fewer meds he took, the more unstable he became. Moody. Argumentative. Angry for no reason…'

She gritted her teeth and half turned away, but not before he glimpsed hardships he never knew had existed. Regret that he hadn't known mingled with anger at his obtuseness, clawing at his gut until he felt as if he were being ripped apart from the inside out.

He didn't want to know how bad it had been but he'd started this, he couldn't back down from the truth now.

'Did he ever hit you?'

His fingers unconsciously curled into fists beneath the table at the thought of his mum possibly enduring physical abuse when he'd had no bloody clue.

She bit her bottom lip, as if she'd already said too much. 'No. But the senseless arguments were hard to take at times.' Her tremulous voice broke his heart but before he could offer useless comfort, her head came up, her defiance admirable. 'I hated your father at times for the way he treated me, but I loved him too. It's why I stayed and told him in no uncertain terms that if he didn't get back on his meds and see a counsellor, I'd kill him myself.'

Shell-shocked, Alex dragged in several deep breaths. It did little to quell the sickening churning of his gut. 'I had no idea.'

'Exactly how I wanted it.' Some of the tension holding her shoulders rigid eased. 'Our marriage wasn't pretty and I'm sorry you were privy to most of it. I tried to hide my bitterness but it spilled out sometimes and your father saw it. Those were the days I wondered if my loyalty and love were misplaced…' She shook her head. 'But I'm a fighter. I stuck around to help him and because I stick by my vows.' She smiled at him. 'You were another very valid reason to stick around. I wanted to give you the home life I never had.'

Fuck, this was crazy. He knew his mum had been a foster kid but to stay in a dead-end marriage with a depressed man because of him? Like he needed any more guilt.

'You shouldn't have put up with him for me.'

Damn, he sounded ungrateful, but she didn't bristle as he expected.

'You don't understand because you don't have a child. When you do, you'll get it.' She placed a hand over her heart. 'What you feel in here? You'll do anything for your child.'

'And I repay you by escaping and never looking back.' He scowled, hating the guilt seeping into every cell of his body. He'd been a selfish bastard, so hellbent on running from his past he hadn't stopped to think what it would be like for those left behind, particularly his mother. 'I'm sorry, Mum. For everything.'

He huffed out a long breath. He'd come this far, he had to tell her the rest. 'I blamed myself for Dad's death for a long time, figuring if I'd made more of an effort to be the son he wanted while I was here that he would've been happier. And later, after I left, that I should've visited more often.'

Her hand trembled as she briefly touched his cheek. 'Your father had a mental illness. We both did as much as we could, so never blame yourself for a decision that was ultimately his to make.'

She smiled and it chased away the darkness of memories shrouding her. He remembered those rare smiles, when she'd look at him with pride and love, like she couldn't quite believe he was hers. He'd loved those smiles. Those brief fragments in time when he could pretend his mum was happy and, in turn, he was too.

She'd done it all out of loyalty. To her marriage, to his father and to him.

He couldn't fathom that depth of caring for another person, maybe he never would.

If having a partner and child meant sacrificing a part of his soul, he wanted no part of it.

Her hand steadied as it cupped his cheek. 'You're a good boy. Always were, even if you have a funny way of showing it.'

He wanted to promise he'd visit more often. That he wouldn't be an absentee son any more. But he didn't intend to make promises he couldn't keep, despite the best intentions, so he settled for divulging the truth considering she'd done him the same courtesy.

'I came home because I met someone and she wants this kind of life.' He screwed up his nose and gestured at the kitchen. 'She wants the house and the garden and the mind-numbing stability. And I needed a reminder of why I'd run away from all that and why I can't share any of that with her.'

His mum tilted her head to one side, studying him with an intensity that unnerved. 'She wants all that other stuff, but does she want you?'

That was the kicker.

He didn't know.

He'd presumed to think she wanted him as part of her happily-ever-after scenario but what if he'd misread the situation? What if she really was happy with a short-term fling, getting all the raunchy stuff out of her system before settling down with some sedate bloke who'd give her the long-term security she craved?

God, he'd been a fool.

And the worst part was, now that he'd come home and talked to his mum, sitting in this kitchen that calmed rather than antagonised, remembering good times more than bad, he realised that having a place to put down roots mightn't be such a bad thing after all.

The thought of being stuck in one place, with one woman, terrified him. The fear of their relationship growing stale, the fear of growing complacent, the fear of drifting apart. His worst frigging nightmare come to life.

It had happened to his folks but now he knew the truth. His father's problems had been organic, stemming from a mental illness, and his mother had stayed by choice. Sure, she'd done it out of love—for him and his father—but to tolerate that kind of a marriage seemed like a massive sacrifice.

Alex didn't have it in him to be so giving. To fall in with another's life plan when he had his own.

But what happened if he kept drifting, until he woke up one day and realised he'd given up a wonderful woman for a life of...nothing?

His mum hadn't run when the going got tough. Maybe spending his whole life running away from possible heartache wasn't the answer for him either?

'I think the expression on your face says it all.' His mum laid her hand on the table, palm up and he didn't hesitate to place his hand in hers. 'Sounds like you've faced a few of your fears in coming back here. Why not go all the way and take a chance on love?'

Alex squeezed her hand, unable to find the words
to respond.

He didn't love.

He couldn't.

But what if he already did?

CHAPTER TWENTY-SIX

YESTERDAY, CHARLOTTE HAD thought it kind of sweet that Alex had been so considerate and given her the day off.

Last night, she'd waited for his call. Or a text. Or something. When she hadn't heard from him, she'd assumed his sweetness extended to being solicitous about her fatigue and leaving her alone to have an early night. Then she'd turned up at work this morning to discover he'd taken two days off, without leaving a word of his whereabouts.

Not so sweet after all.

It shouldn't bother her because technically they weren't in a committed relationship and he didn't need to check in with her regarding his whereabouts. But it did. Which proved how involved she really was despite all her assertions to the contrary.

Only one way to get him out of her head: focus on work.

She'd hardly been in the office for thirty minutes and all the talk centred around promotions. Her co-workers insisted she was a shoo-in for the new managerial role and while she feigned bashfulness she knew deep down they were right.

She'd completed every task Alex had set her before

he'd arrived in Sydney. She'd gone the extra yard for clients. She'd gone above and beyond in all aspects of new case files.

She deserved this promotion.

If he announced it when he got back she wouldn't hesitate to make a deposit on her house. She could hardly wait.

'Where's the Proudman file?' she called out to the receptionist when she couldn't find it on her desk.

'Alex was working on it before he left.' The receptionist jerked her thumb towards his office. 'It's probably still on his desk.'

'Thanks.' Charlotte breezed into Alex's office like it was the most natural thing in the world when every time she set foot in here her heart started pounding and bucking like a wild thing.

That desk...

Even after he left she'd never be able to look at it without blushing. Never in her wildest dreams had she thought she could be the type of woman who had sex on a desk, let alone at her workplace. But she'd gone kind of crazy the moment she'd met Alex and the insanity hadn't let up since.

She hated contemplating the end of their fling but it had served its purpose. Being awakened sexually, feeling confident in her own skin when it came to men, would ensure she could socialise and date without gaucheness. After all, she'd have the house soon enough, a solid, dependable man had to follow.

When she found herself inadvertently running her hands over the desk she shook her head to clear her musings and started searching for the Proudman file. Alex must have left in a hurry because files were stacked on top of documents in disarray, with seemingly no order to any of it.

She started tidying up, putting the files on one side, documents on the other in a neat pile. A heading on one of the documents snagged her attention. *Promotions.*

She shouldn't look at it. She wouldn't. But curiosity got the better of her and she risked a quick glance. And froze.

He'd listed promotions in order from managerial positions down.

Her name wasn't at the top.

He'd given her job, the one she'd busted her ass to get, to Dennis, the guy she'd mentored when he first arrived three years ago.

In what warped, twisted world did some guy with less experience than her get to be her boss for the foreseeable future?

Anger surged through her, making her fingers flex and the paper crinkle. Damn. She quickly smoothed it out and slid it to the bottom of the pile, sorting faster through the files until she found the one she wanted.

Alex had given her job to someone else when he'd hinted several times it would be hers.

Was he punishing her somehow?

If so, for what?

Anger soon gave way to a familiar emotion, one that consistently rattled her confidence and made her feel unworthy.

Undeserving.

Yet again she'd done her best but had been found lacking. And this time, because she'd been stupid enough to drag her bruised heart into the equation, the fallout would be so much worse.

Like her parents, Alex had deemed her not good enough.

It cut deep, all the way down to her soul.

Shaken to her core, she returned to her office. Sat at her desk. Pretended to work when in fact she spent the next hour staring out of the window envisaging all the ways she could punish her boss.

Starting with ending this thing between them.

What had she been thinking, to indulge in a brief, irrational and futile affair that could only end badly?

Now, not only would she have to deal with a pining heart—because yeah, she'd been stupid enough to fall for him a little—she'd have to tolerate working beneath a guy who had the promotion she deserved.

'Crap,' she muttered, thumping her desk with both fists. It did little but make her hands sting. Better than her eyes, as she dragged in several breaths to stave off tears.

This was what came of harbouring hopes.

This was what came of fooling herself into believing things could be different this time, that she'd be enough, that she wouldn't be found lacking.

She'd been a fool.

But no more.

The moment Alex got back, they were O.V.E.R.

CHAPTER TWENTY-SEVEN

ALEX WISHED HE'D had the balls to confront his past earlier. He'd never felt so light, as if a weight had been lifted from his shoulders. Seeing his mother, getting answers to questions that had plagued him for years, had ensured he had a clearer vision for the future.

He didn't have to shy away from commitment for fear of ending up like his folks.

He just had to change the boundaries of what would make a relationship work for him.

As he stood outside Charlotte's flat and waited for her to answer his knock, he rocked on the balls of his feet, excitement making him edgy.

He hadn't bothered texting her when his plane had landed. He'd wanted to surprise her.

The proposal he had for her was that damn monumental. Huge. Life-changing. If she agreed.

She would. He'd do everything in his power to convince her.

He knew she felt more for him than she let on. He'd seen it in her eyes so many times. And in the way she'd opened up to him about her hopes and dreams.

They could make this work. He had no doubt. They both just needed to have a little faith.

She took an eternity to answer and he knocked again, louder this time. When she finally opened the door, all the air whooshed out of his lungs.

She wore a towel. A large bath sheet that hid more than it revealed, but he knew what was beneath it and that was enough to drive all rational thought from his head.

'Hey,' she said, but he didn't give her time to say much else as he entered, kicked the door shut and reached for her.

He glimpsed wariness in her eyes—she was probably mad at him for taking off without letting her know where—and something far scarier. Sadness. As if she knew their time together was coming to an end.

Not if he had his way, so he set about showing her just how special she was to him.

He hauled her into his arms and crushed his mouth to hers, savouring the way she instantly opened to him, their tongues tangling as if they hadn't kissed in years. It had only been a few days but it felt like for ever and he slid his hands under her towel, grabbed her ass and hoisted her up.

She made cute mewling sounds as he turned and backed her up against the door. Small whimpers of appreciation when he slipped a hand between them to touch her clit, the swollen nub slick already.

Their kiss deepened to the point he couldn't breathe. He didn't care, as his thumb circled that nub with precision, until she came apart on a loud moan.

Her hands clutched at his shoulders as he sheathed himself and slid into her, her welcoming tightness something he'd never tire of. As if she were made for him.

His fingers dug into her ass as he lifted her higher,

changing the angle, making him a little insane as he drove into her. She wrapped her legs around his waist, squeezing him tight and a groan ripped from somewhere deep inside.

Every thrust, every plunge, took him closer to the edge. Too fast. Not fast enough. The exquisite friction of his cock inside her set off a reaction that blanked his mind until all he could focus on was her. This. Now.

At some point his mouth had drifted across her jaw, to her ear, where he murmured exactly what he was feeling at that moment. 'I could fuck you like this for ever.'

With a strangled cry, she angled her head and claimed his mouth, her back arching, her pelvis moulded to his. It was enough to drive him over the edge, the white-hot explosion of heat behind his eyeballs blinding him to everything as he came harder than ever before.

She sagged against him, limp in his arms. He held her close, knowing with a certainty he could never walk away from her, no matter how much the thought of anything long-term freaked him out.

When his arms started to ache from holding her up, he gently eased back so she had no option but to lower her legs to the floor. She'd lost the towel at some stage, leaving her gloriously naked. He took a moment to appreciate her creamy expanses of skin, her taut nipples, her perfect breasts.

'God, you're beautiful,' he said, brushing a kiss across her lips. 'Be back in a minute.'

He cleaned up in the bathroom, splashed some water on his face to wash off the plane journey and by the time he came back out she sat perched on the edge of an armchair, fully clothed in yoga pants and a hoodie.

'I much prefer you in that towel,' he said, sitting on
the sofa and patting the empty spot next to him.

When she didn't move, he realised she hadn't spoken
a single word since he'd arrived.

'Are you okay?'

'I'm fine.'

She didn't sound it, her voice tight and controlled.
'Busy day and I'm beat.'

'Same.' He ignored the faintest clang of alarm bells
in his head. Usually after they'd had scintillating sex
she'd be all over him, wanting to touch and cuddle.
Today, her stiff posture and thinned lips were giving
him a distinct hands-off signal.

She was mad at him for taking off without an explanation, so he'd give her one.

'I flew home for a few days. A last-minute trip. Sorry
for not telling you.'

One eyebrow raised a fraction. 'You don't owe me
any explanations.'

Ouch. She really was pissed.

So he continued. 'I needed to see Mum, clarify a
few things.'

'Good.' A brief, one-syllable response that sounded
far from it.

'I came straight here from the airport because I want
to ask you something.'

He took a deep breath.

Here goes nothing.

'When I leave Sydney I want you to come with me.
Live on the road for a while. Share a few adventures…'
He trailed off when she stared at him in open-mouthed
shock, and not the good kind.

She looked seriously annoyed, as if he'd inconvenienced her somehow, her stare bordering on loathing.

Fuck.

Had he misread their relationship? Had he got the situation all wrong?

He'd assumed she felt like him, that she'd want more beyond a short-term fling. His offer, to have her become a part of his life, was the closest he'd ever come to a long-term commitment with a woman.

Facing his fears rooted in the past had liberated him, had given him the courage to embrace a new future, with her.

But what if she didn't want him?

'Say something,' he said, hating the hint of desperation in his tone.

She clasped her hands in her lap so tightly her knuckles stood out, a frown slashing her brows. 'Is that why you did it?'

'Did what?'

'You're going to appoint Dennis Boage to the managerial position so I'll be more likely to chuck in my job and come travelling with you on a whim?'

She didn't shout. He could have handled irrational anger if she'd yelled. But her cold, frosty tone scared him as much as the bleakness in her eyes.

'What are you talking about?'

'I saw it!' She leaped to her feet, finally showing some sign of defiance. 'Your list of promotions, with my name beneath his.'

She stalked around the coffee table to stand over him, hands on hips, magnificent in her ire. 'You know how much that promotion means to me, how much owning that house means to me, then you go and pull something like this?'

He stood slowly, disbelief warring with indignation. Did she think so little of him that she'd believe him capable of messing with her career to suit himself?

'You think this is some kind of stunt?' It was his turn to rein in his anger as icy-cold disdain flooded his veins. 'I came here straight from the airport because I couldn't wait to be with you, to ask you to continue this amazing connection we share. And what do I get? Accusations.'

He muttered, 'Fuck me,' under his breath, unable to comprehend he'd read this situation so wrong.

This was why he didn't do emotional commitment. Ever.

'Maybe if you hadn't gone snooping on my desk, you would've been more amenable to my proposition?' She stiffened at his jibe and he continued. 'Or maybe not, considering you think so little of me.'

He shook his head. 'That document you saw? It was a list I'd made in the early days when I accepted the job. Decisions made purely on recommendations from the old manager. But I don't work like that. I told you so.' He thumped his chest. 'I make my own decisions. You saw me do it. I evaluated everyone fairly. Including you.'

He jabbed a finger in her direction. 'You said you were fine with us having a fling outside work. You said it wouldn't blur any lines.'

He backed away from her, her stony expression shattering what little hope he harboured. 'I call bullshit. Because I've definitely kept work and play separate. Can you say the same?'

He strode for the door, willing her to say something, anything, that would resolve this. Waiting for her to say he'd got it wrong. That she did care for him. That she'd love to travel and have adventures and be his partner for however long.

When he reached the door, she still hadn't spoken.

So he walked away from her without looking back.

CHAPTER TWENTY-EIGHT

THE INITIAL NUMBNESS that invaded Charlotte's body after Alex left soon gave way to tremors, the kind of shaking that made her flop onto the sofa and hug herself tight.

Light-headedness made the room spin a little and nausea made her stomach gripe.

She felt sick, like she'd ingested rotten sushi, something she'd inadvertently done once and had never forgotten. That bout of food poisoning hadn't made her chest ache, though. She could barely breathe through the pain constricting her lungs, like a band around her ribs progressively tightening.

Alex had come here to offer her the world.

She'd flung it back in his face.

She'd never forget his expression once he'd told her the truth.

Total and utter contempt.

The tears she'd been holding back trickled down her cheeks. The second time in a week she'd bawled. So much for her deeming it a wasted activity when it was much better to get on with the job. Set goals. Work hard. Don't lament a lack of a family/boyfriend/love life.

But she'd never felt like this before. Bereft. Aching. Grieving for the loss of something—someone—wonderful.

Her laptop beeped on the table, the screen lighting up to indicate she had an incoming video call. From her parents.

Crap.

They rarely called her. Except the obligatory birthday and Christmas. So this call out of the blue could only mean one thing.

Trouble.

She stared at the screen, tempted to ignore the call. But the unexpectedness of it made her anxious and she didn't need one more thing to worry about when she lay awake all night.

Dabbing at her eyes with the hem of her hoodie, she squared her shoulders. She could do this. She'd made an art form of feigning indifference towards her parents for many years, pretending their abandonment didn't hurt.

She stabbed at the answer button and waited for their faces to appear on the screen. Where were they at the moment? Spain? Morocco? Nepal? She lost track of their destinations after a while, only giving their postcards a cursory glance before stuffing them into a box.

Initially they'd given her such joy as a child, cards featuring interesting pictures from exotic locations. She'd run to the mailbox every day in the hope to receive one. But as time passed and her parents didn't return she'd grown to hate those postcards, tangible proof of her two closest biological links not giving a crap about her.

She could count the number of times they'd flown back to Sydney to visit her on one hand. They'd left her with Dee the day after her sixth birthday and had returned at two-yearly intervals, usually staying a week max, until she'd turned sixteen. By then she hadn't been able to hide her dislike and they'd stopped visiting.

But those frigging postcards still arrived like clockwork. No digital correspondence for them. Were they truly that clueless, that they couldn't comprehend how each and every one of those little cardboard rectangles acted like a knife to her heart, a reminder of how they'd turned their back on their only child?

Their faces finally appeared on the screen and she forced a smile. 'Hey, nomads.'

She rarely called them Mum and Dad these days. It didn't feel right as they were so far from being parental it wasn't funny.

'Hi, darling.'

Another falsity. They always called her darling and it grated as badly now as it had in her teens.

Quashing her residual bitterness, she said, 'Is everything okay?'

'Everything's fine,' her mum said, not looking a day older than the last time they'd video-called five months ago. Her blonde hair had a few streaks of grey but her hazel eyes fairly sparkled with joy. Half her luck. 'We just thought we'd call and tell you our news.'

Charlotte's heart sank. She'd grown immune to her parents' 'news' over the years, which usually revolved around them trying to conquer some new far-flung destination.

'What news?'

Did they believe she genuinely sounded upbeat or could they tell she faked it? After what had happened with Alex, she didn't care. Her life was falling apart and they didn't have a clue because they hadn't been around long enough to get a read on their own daughter.

'We've been awarded a grant to open a small school in Papua New Guinea.' Her mother leaned into her father, who stared down at her like she hung the moon. 'It's an incredible opportunity to work with the kids there and the best part is, we're closer to you.'

Her mum rubbed her hands together as her dad leaned towards the screen. 'Isn't that great? We can pop in for a visit more often. See our best girl.'

A long-festering resentment burned her gut. Their best girl? She was their only girl and they'd never given a crap about her.

'We miss you, darling.' Her mum blew her a kiss, her dad doing the same a moment later. 'Maybe you could come and visit us? See what we do? Get a feel for the sacrifice we made in leaving you behind but how much we've helped those less fortunate?'

As they both stared at her with such unabashed happiness, Charlotte felt the first stirrings of something akin to yearning.

What would it be like to live life to the fullest like her parents? To want to do good for others? To not care about owning possessions or saving for the future? To live out of a suitcase, unconcerned about mortgage repayments or bills or superannuation?

She'd always scoffed at their lifestyle, believing them to be frivolous and foolish in their inability to plan for the future. She'd labelled them selfish for following their own path and abandoning her to do it.

But hearing them say they'd actually made a sacrifice to leave her behind to help others less fortunate resonated.

She'd never considered that. She'd been too absorbed in her self-pity party for one, attributing their gadding about to selfishness, not selflessness.

How she'd yearned for normal parents growing up. Parents who attended information nights. Parents who pretended to be the Easter bunny, tooth fairy and Santa. Parents who gave a damn.

Dee adored her, always had, and the feeling was entirely mutual. She hadn't wanted for anything and her aunt had become the mother she'd never had. But no matter how nurturing Dee had been, Charlotte had never been able to get past the fact that her own parents preferred caring for strangers rather than their own child.

'Is everything okay?' Her dad leaned closer to the screen again, a habit she found endearing at times. 'You look upset.'

'I'm fine, Dad.'

But she saw the look her folks exchanged, as if they didn't buy her excuse for a second. Great timing for them to suddenly discover the parental gene.

'How's work?' her mum prompted, her usual inquiry whenever they spoke. They didn't have much else in common and her mum had discovered early on not to ask about her social life—or lack of one.

'Fine.'

'That's your second fine in thirty seconds.' Her dad waggled his finger at her. 'A sure sign you're not.'

Charlotte had no intention of divulging the mess she'd made of her love life so she changed the subject. 'Tell me more about this project in Papua New Guinea.'

It worked like magic, her parents taking it in turns to tell her about the school they envisaged, growing increasingly animated as they spoke.

Charlotte barely heard half of what they said, too busy watching their body language. They constantly touched, leaned into each other and finished each other's sentences. Her dad kissed her mum twice, once on the top of her head as she snuggled into him, once on her cheek when she gazed up at him in adoration.

That was when it hit her.

Maybe them travelling the world together hadn't been about abandoning her at all.

Maybe they didn't need anyone else in their lives, they were that connected.

How many couples still appeared so in love after twenty-nine years of marriage? She couldn't think of any. Her co-workers constantly bitched about their spouses and Dee had divorced at twenty-four after eighteen months of marriage.

Yet here were her folks, appearing truly happy in their life choices. She might never forgive them for abandoning her, for choosing their lifestyle over her, but it made her realise something.

Their enthusiasm for life shone through in their words and actions. They practically glowed with it.

She'd made it her goal to be the opposite of them, to do the opposite. Choose security and stability and a house over travel and adventure. Build a nest egg rather than squander what little money she had. Find a staid, dependable man and have a relationship based on trust and friendship rather than any grand passion.

She'd had it all planned out.

So why did she feel like she'd short-changed herself somehow?

Maybe she should be trying to emulate her parents' marriage and lifestyle, not shy from it?

Alex had offered her the opportunity and she'd rejected it. For a guy who'd been totally upfront about not doing long-term commitment, it must have taken a big turnaround for him to ask her to go with him.

She'd been so damn angry at the time, so sure he was dangling a relationship in front of her to make up for the fact he'd taken away her promotion and thus affected her future mortgage and dream house.

But what if she was wrong?

What if Alex had asked her to accompany him on his travels because he felt their connection went far deeper than sex?

She felt it. Why couldn't he?

'I think your plans sound wonderful, Mum and Dad, but I have to go. Sorry. We'll chat soon.'

And she meant it, disconnecting before they could ramble on further.

She had things to do. Important things.

Starting with showing Alex that she *was* the kind of woman to take risks.

CHAPTER TWENTY-NINE

ALEX HAD DONE many impulsive things in his lifetime.

Buying a house wasn't one of them.

But he had to do this, because if he didn't he'd lose Charlie completely and that wasn't possible.

After he'd stormed out of her flat, he'd driven aimlessly, determined to clear his head. He'd taken a wrong turn down one of Sydney's infamous one-way streets and ended up having to go over the Harbour Bridge to Manly. He parked, slipped off his shoes and socks, rolled up his trousers and walked along the beach. Something guys in suits rarely did by the number of odd glances garnered from passers-by.

He had no idea if it was the fresh sea air, the feel of sand between his toes or the simple art of walking for pleasure rather than as a means to get somewhere, but by the time he got back to his car his anger had given way to determination.

He'd shied away from commitment his entire life. He'd made many excuses, mostly to himself, not to get emotionally involved with a woman. But he wanted to have more than a fling with Charlotte and if she hadn't accepted his first offer, this time he'd make her an offer too good to refuse.

She valued stability, he didn't.

What if he could meet her halfway?

It took him two hours to get the deal done. Sign the paperwork. Make it legit, so he could present her with tangible proof of how far he was willing to go for her.

He had no idea if he'd ever tread down the marriage road—he couldn't shed all his neuroses at once—but admitting he loved her would be a good start. It would be enough for now.

With the relevant documents tucked firmly in his breast pocket, he hightailed it back to her flat.

To find a decrepit set of three suitcases outside her door.

Fuck. The sight of those forlorn cases almost undid him. She was leaving? Maybe she really didn't love him after all?

A steely resolve he'd used many times in the business arena overran his momentary doubts.

Only one way to find out how she felt, once and for all.

He pounded on the door, surprised to find it swung open.

'Charlie?' he called out, entering the quiet flat.

'In here,' she answered, her voice drifting from behind the semi-closed bedroom door.

After shutting the front door, he went in search of her. He pushed the bedroom door open and stopped when he saw the bomb site that her bedroom had become.

Piles of clothes lay in disarray on the floor. Shoes covered any unused space. And three designer suitcases bearing a renowned emblem took pride of place on the bed, open and ready to be stuffed.

'Going somewhere?' He gestured at the cases, his heart sinking. Had she started packing for the move to her dream house?

'Yeah.' She flung a plain grey dress that had seen better days onto a pile behind her.

'Where?'

'Not sure yet,' she said, shooting him an uncertain glance. 'That depends on you.'

'Me?'

He couldn't acknowledge the tiny flare of hope. Not yet. He'd already made the mistake of assuming too much and look where that had got him. Absolutely nowhere.

'Well, I couldn't very well accompany you on an adventure with those tatty old cases so I invested a sizeable chunk of my house deposit on new luggage.' She gestured to the cases on the bed. 'So you'd better still take me on your travels, otherwise I'll be stuck with these very expensive pieces and nowhere to go.'

Alex could have whooped for joy.

She felt it too. This crazy, indescribable, heady feeling that defied belief or explanation. The kind of feeling that prompted them to do outlandish things, like squander her house deposit on designer luggage. Like him buying a house.

'I'm taking you wherever I go,' he said, aiming for nonchalance as he slid the sale documents out of his pocket and handed them to her. 'But first, you might like to take a look at this.'

'Airline tickets?' Her soft smile shot something straight to his heart, something that lodged and he'd never be able to shake off.

This incredible woman was willing to give up her

dreams to be with him. He'd make damn sure he was
worthy of her faith in him.

'No. Check it out.'

She unfolded the paper, her eyes scanning it quickly
and he saw the exact moment reality hit.

'You didn't,' she whispered, her hands shaking a
tad as she re-read the document, then let out an ear-
piercing squeal. 'You bought my dream house and put
it in my name?'

'Yeah. Seeing as you doubted my intentions, I had to
do something outrageous to prove how much I love you.'

'You love me…' she murmured, shaking her head as
if to clear it. 'I can't believe this.'

'Believe it, babe,' he said, kicking clothes out of the
way to get to her. 'This way, you'll always have the
house. And who knows, maybe one day you'll let me
live in it with you. But in the meantime, let's go wild.
Take some time off. Travel. Have fun.' He stopped two
feet in front of her, yearning to take her in his arms.
'Knowing that you'll have a managerial role when you
get back to The Number Makers.'

Her bottom lip wobbled and tears filled her eyes.
'You are the most incredible man I've ever known and
I can't thank you enough for all you've done for me.'

'Pfft. Buying a house is nothing—'

'I'm not talking about the house and you know it.'
She stepped forward and rested her palms against his
chest, staring up at him in wonder. 'You've awakened
me sexually. You've given me self-confidence. You've
made me feel worthy for the first time in my life. And
most of all you've made me take a risk and fall in love
with a wanderer.'

He grinned like an idiot. 'So you love me too, huh?'

'Oh, yeah, and I intend to prove it every which way in every city in every country we visit.' She slid her palms up slowly, to cup his face. 'And don't worry, I'm not packing anything but kinky lingerie.'

He laughed, wrapped his arms around her waist, picked her up and swung her around until they were both dizzy.

When they came to a stop, he rested his forehead against hers. 'My very own play thing, complete with raunchy accessories. How did I get so lucky?'

'You're about to get a whole lot luckier,' she said, moving the suitcases off the bed before pushing him onto it and straddling him. 'For the rest of your life, if you'll have me.'

'So I'm your dream man?' He propped himself up on his elbows, watching with lascivious intent as she peeled off her T-shirt and flung it onto the floor.

'You're every dream and fantasy I've ever had rolled into one.' She unclipped her bra at the back and it followed the same route as her T-shirt, leaving her delectable breasts bare to him. 'And I can't wait to share every adventure together.'

He reached for her, wanting her to fill his hands the way she'd filled his heart. 'Starting now...'

* * * * *

COMING SOON!

We really hope you enjoyed reading this book. If you're looking for more romance, be sure to head to the shops when new books are available on

Thursday
1st November

To see which titles are coming soon, please visit
millsandboon.co.uk

MILLS & BOON

LET'S TALK
Romance

For exclusive extracts, competitions
and special offers, find us online:

f facebook.com/millsandboon

⊙ @millsandboonuk

🐦 @millsandboon

Or get in touch on 0844 844 1351*

For all the latest titles coming soon, visit
millsandboon.co.uk/nextmonth

Want even more
ROMANCE?

Join our bookclub today!

'Mills & Boon books, the perfect way to escape for an hour or so.'

Miss W. Dyer

'Excellent service, promptly delivered and very good subscription choices.'

Miss A. Pearson

'You get fantastic special offers and the chance to get books before they hit the shops'

Mrs V. Hall

Visit millsandbook.co.uk/Bookclub
and save on brand new books.

MILLS & BOON